Love and Romanpunk
Tansy Rayner Roberts

First published in Australia in May 2011
by Twelfth Planet Press

www.twelfthplanetpress.com

All works © 2011 Tansy Rayner Roberts
Design and layout by Amanda Rainey
Typeset in Sabon MT Pro

All rights reserved. Without limiting the rights under copyright above, no part of this publication may be reproduced, stored in or introduced into a retrieval system, or transmitted in any form, or by any means (electronic, mechanical, photocopying, recording or otherwise), without the prior written permission of both the copyright owner and the above publisher of this book.

National Library of Australia Cataloguing-in-Publication entry

Author: Roberts, Tansy Rayner, 1978-

Title: Love and Romanpunk : a Twelve Planets collection /
           by Tansy Rayner Roberts, edited by Alisa Krasnostein.

ISBN: 9780980827446 (pbk.)

Other Authors/Contributors:
           Krasnostein, Alisa.

Dewey Number: A823.3

*For Random Alex, who needs more romanpunk
in her life, even though she is completely wrong to love
Marc Antony more than Octavian.*

Really, really wrong.

Also From
Twelfth Planet Press

ANTHOLOGIES / COLLECTIONS:

2012, edited by Alisa Krasnostein and Ben Payne

New Ceres Nights, edited by Alisa Krasnostein and Tehani Wessely

A Book of Endings, by Deborah Biancotti

Glitter Rose, by Marianne de Pierres

Sprawl, edited by Alisa Krasnostein

Nightsiders, by Sue Isle

NOVELLA SERIES:

Angel Rising, by Dirk Flinthart

Horn, by Peter M. Ball

Siren Beat, by Tansy Rayner Roberts /
Roadkill, by Robert Shearman

Bleed, by Peter M. Ball

The Company Articles of Edward Teach, by Thoraiya Dyer /
The Angælien Apocalypse, by Matthew Crulew

Above, by Stephanie Campisi /
Below, by Ben Peek

Contents

Introduction	1
Julia Agrippina's Secret Family Bestiary	3
Lamia Victoriana	39
The Patrician	51
Last of the Romanpunks	79
Afterword	105
About the Author	107
Acknowledgements	109

Introduction

One of the best things about the Twelve Planets series—apart from the fact that it showcases some amazingly talented Australian authors—is the freedom it gives both writer and reader to discover, to explore, to play, and to chance unexpected encounters.

Love and Romanpunk offers just such a delightful and surprising encounter with quite a different face of the multi-talented Tansy Rayner Roberts. You may know Rayner Roberts as the George Turner-award winning YA author, or an accomplished short story writer, or the author of the acclaimed Creature Court fantasy trilogy. Some of you may know her as the erudite blogger, book critic or feminist podcaster. What you may not know is her love of all things Roman, and the fact she has a PhD in Roman history. I see this collection as a super-collision of the potentialities of the Rayner Roberts continuum which, not coincidently, requires a whole new subgenre. And its name is Romanpunk.

What, you may well ask, is Romanpunk? Take a solid grounding in Roman history and mythology, add a sense of humour, love of urban fantasy, a penchant for Bronze swords, and you are getting close. While the intent of the label is partly in jest, the execution is anything but. This is someone who knows their Roman history, knows their spec-fic and is, happily, well-equipped to bring a very different take on the vampires that over-haunt contemporary urban fantasy.

Think Connie Willis meets Gail Carriger over much more than a cup of tea.

And true to the Twelve Planets remit, this is a clearly feminist re-making of genre: a loving but passionately critical reclamation of the tired old vampire subject, of the women of Roman history, of urban fantasy, of unrequited teenage love and doomed Romantic relationships. Work in some serious history lessons and you'll start to understand that this slim volume packs a lot of punch.

All of the stories are satisfying in their own right, together forming a fascinating chronicle of a past and future where mythological beasts are far from mythical, and the name Julia resonates with particular power. For me, 'The Patrician' stands out as being close to the perfect short story. Starting with just the right sort of frissons of cognitive dissonance that make clear this is not quite *our* world, the story draws you into absolute complicity with its alternate history and latter-day love story, gently depositing you at the end feeling not a little bereft. It made me laugh, it made me cry, and then made me go off and look up some Roman history. What more could a good feminist historian ask for?

For the rest of you, there's a rollercoaster ride over 2000 years of fantastical future history, with lamias (that's Roman vampires to you), warriors, empresses, and famous poets. And perhaps the odd Patricide, Fratricide (it is Rome, after all), and grandmother joke.

Oh, and airships (that's the punk part).

And did I mention it's funny?

Helen Merrick

Julia Agrippina's Secret Family Bestiary

BY JULIA AGRIPPINA MINOR

WIDOW OF TIBERIUS CLAUDIUS NERO

MOTHER OF THE EMPEROR NERO

WIDOW AND NIECE OF THE EMPEROR CLAUDIUS

SISTER OF THE EMPEROR CALIGULA, AND OF JULIA DRUSILLA, JULIA LIVILLA, NERO AND DRUSUS

DAUGHTER OF AGRIPPINA MAJOR AND GERMANICUS CAESAR

GRANDDAUGHTER OF JULIA MAJOR AND MARCUS VIPSANIUS AGRIPPA

GREAT-GRANDDAUGHTER OF THE EMPEROR AUGUSTUS

ENEMY OF LIVIA DRUSILLA, WIFE OF AUGUSTUS, BITCH OF ROME

Love and Romanpunk   *Tansy Rayner Roberts*

Let us begin with the issue of most interest to future historians: I did not poison my uncle and husband, the Emperor Claudius. Instead, I drove a stake through his heart.

In my defence, several of my close relatives have been vampires, and I have had little occasion to kill any of them. Claudius was a particular case.

For the sake of good scholarship, I have arranged the secrets of my family in alphabetical order, beast by beast.

Basilisk
I was four years old when a basilisk tried to kill my brother. Caligula was unimportant then; we had a father and two elder brothers who were in line to be Uncle Tiberius' heirs, and Caligula was a skinny little drip of a thing, eleven years old and not nearly as pretty as he had been as a small child when the soldiers made him their good luck charm.

We lived on the march, following our famous father from army camp to army camp. We were used to sand in our clothes and rain in our hair.

I woke early, and smelled smoke. I crawled over Drusilla's sleeping form and stuck my head out of the tent in time to see the nearby bushes burst into flame and ash. I cried out to warn the camp and soldiers ran here and there, drawing swords and routing the monsters.

My mother and siblings ran out too, all but Caligula, who yawned and turned in his bedroll, and my baby sister Julia, asleep in her cradle.

A dark stain appeared on the back of our tent, blackening the canvas, and then a hole burned through. The creature crawled inside, balancing its serpentine, slithery body on two spiky bird feet.

I learned later that if the basilisk had met my gaze, I would have died in an instant. Luckily, its attention was entirely taken up by my lazy, slumbering brother.

Later, my mother also expressed surprise that I had managed to fling my sister's wooden rattle with such force that it had pierced the creature instantly through the neck.

My father (how I loved him in that moment) shrugged and smiled. 'After all,' he said, 'she is a Julia.'

Centaur

To be a Julia meant something long before our family became Emperors and gods. Julius Caesar, the conqueror, once gave a fine funeral speech for his Aunt Julia, the wife of Marius, paying particular attention to the time she had saved her husband's army from being attacked by centaurs without setting foot outside her weaving room in Rome. It was she who had sent Marius a pouch of lucky seeds which, when scattered on the earth around their campsite, turned overnight into sharp-thorned caltraps.

The women of our family have ever been fierce, and effective. It is said that upon the death of Marius, it was Julia who guarded his grave from magicians who would have stolen a bone or lock of hair to fuel war charms, or *virilis* potions.

There is a carving of Julia upon her tomb that shows her protecting her dead husband, his *gladius* in one hand and her own wicked-sharp spindle in the other.

***

Love and Romanpunk   *Tansy Rayner Roberts*

Dragon

Everyone knows that weaving is women's work. When my great-grandfather Augustus, first Emperor of Rome, came to power, he declared far and wide that the women of his family were the most virtuous, the most hard-working. Why, every garment on his back had been woven by his womenfolk: his wife Livia and daughter Julia.

Livia indeed had an entire hall of slaves who ensured that she was able to provide her husband with homespun weaving.

Julia's skills lay elsewhere—she could ride a horse as well as a man, draw a bow with the strength of an Amazon, discuss literature with searing intelligence, and flirt the greatest of secrets out of any ambassador, armed only with a glass of red wine and a warm smile. But her father's values were old-fashioned, and he did not wish the Julias of the imperial family to emulate the warrior women of our family's past.

He wanted his daughter to weave. And so, though she would have been more useful in the army at her husband's side, or protecting the body of her father, or charming the visitors from Egypt and Jerusalem, Julia worked in wool, over and over, perfecting the skills her father valued.

This was her life for many years. She married Agrippa, bore him several children, and worked in wool. She was only one day a widow when her father gave her into another marriage, this time to her stepbrother, Tiberius, whom no woman could possibly have been expected to tolerate, let alone love.

When Julia was caught astride the son of Mark Antony, persuading him to abandon his treasonous plots even as she fucked him into oblivion, her father did not care that she was entertaining her lovers upon an intricate blanket she had woven herself, with the skills she had built over decades.

Weaving was no longer enough to save her.

Augustus ordered Julia's exile, refusing to see her for the rest of his life. She realised for the first time what he had become, and how little she meant to him as anything but a political tool.

Julia tore her blanket and favourite stola into strips and wove herself a pair of wings, so that she could soar above the city under her own power. By the time she had reached the island nominated as her place of exile, she had built a fine layer of green, hard skin around her limbs, and the hair she was always so vain about had fallen away into the sea.

For the rest of her natural life, Julia looked forward to the day her father would come to beg her forgiveness, so that she could frighten him with the flame that now burst from between her lips, sear his pasty skin with the white hot steam that gushed from her nostrils, and then could finally lay her new body aside and be a woman once more.

But he never came, and in time she preferred to be a dragon. No one expected her to do anything with her claws except that which was mighty and fearsome. Julia had always wanted to be fearsome.

Eagle

When Augustus died, it was not Julia's sons who inherited Rome. Each of them had fallen, from poisoned wounds or mysterious illnesses. It was Tiberius, son of Livia, who took the Empire. One of his first duties was to make Augustus a god.

We Romans are a people of many gods. Adding more to the pantheon is a common tradition. Yet, to the Julian family, this moment was vital, and the pursuit of godhood was to remain a familial obsession for generations to come. Livia craved it. My brother Caligula dreamed of it. My uncle and husband Claudius dreaded it, I think.

To become a god was to be an eagle, soaring above the city. I was born one year into the reign of Tiberius, and my brothers would often tease me by pointing out the birds in flight, hollering, 'There he is, Augustus is watching you!' They made me cry out of fear that the old man would fly down and peck out my eyes.

Years later, I played the same trick on my own younger sisters.

What is it, to be a god? Surely it means something more than a diadem upon a marble statue. I imagine a dusty room in which my brother, uncle-husband, step-grandfather and great-grandfather sit around in fine robes, pecking at crumbs like the birds that flock around the temples.

What can they possibly have to say to each other?

Griffin

When the first imperial Julia winged her way into exile in the body of the dragon, she left behind two living daughters. Agrippina, who was to be my mother, and Julia Minor, also called Julilla.

The first Julia had been blonde, fair of face, with curves even the unflattering stola could not disguise. Her daughters were of a different type altogether: they took after their father Agrippa, stocky creatures with dark hair and a soldier's build.

My mother made her escape by winning the heart of Germanicus, nephew of Tiberius, and Livia's golden boy. He was drawn to the maiden with the heart of a warrior, and the two of them left Rome in haste, making a life of army camps and battlefields, defending the Emperor Augustus's borders even as they kept themselves at a safe distance from the Emperor himself.

Julilla, the warrior maid left behind, was not so lucky. The husband arranged for her was not enamoured of a wife who could wrestle a lion or race a pack of hounds. Like her mother before her, she was obliged to spend much of her time working in wool and perfecting other womanly arts.

When it was all too much for her, she would disguise herself as a man and sneak out to the Field of Mars outside the city, where there were always soldiers to train against, to perfect her skills.

One summer, when Rome was at its hottest, a legion of Germanicus' men brought home a gift for the Emperor Augustus: a wild griffin from the desert. Augustus and Livia were holidaying at Capri, and the soldiers were obliged to wait out a long, hot month with a screeching, hostile creature scratching at its cage on the Field of Mars.

It was perhaps inevitable, once flagons of wine entered the equation, that the men should think of fighting the beast.

They sent in their toughest wrestlers and boxers to combat the creature, mindful that they dare not use swords, for the griffin must remain intact for the Emperor. The game then was how long you could stay in the circle drawn in the sand around the creature, which was cuffed to a stake by one leg to restrict its own movements.

To stay inside for ten beats of the drum earned you a cup of wine. Twenty beats earned you wine and an ovation by your fellow men. Thirty would win you a purse of gold, but none of them had managed thirty yet except for young Gaius who was killed at the eighth beat, and only stayed inside so long because none of them could figure out how to safely drag his body free.

Have you ever seen a griffin? It is one of those creatures apparently formed from several others, by some arcane hand. It has the head and wings of an eagle and the body of a lion, and is utterly vicious.

Under other circumstances, Julilla, the youngest granddaughter of Augustus, might have allowed the challenge to pass, but it had been a tiresome summer full of dull dinner parties, and she was so sick of her husband's droning, pious verse that she feared one day she might snap and bite his throat out.

Instead, she put on the masculine guise of Barefisted Lillus, and went out to the field to drink and fight with the soldiers. Thus she found herself within a circle of sand, dodging and weaving as the monster bit and snarled and lunged at her. She moved around and around, careful to let it choke itself on its own chain, and landed at least one punch before it unfurled itself with an exasperated cry and caught her in the chest with a claw the length of a bread knife.

When Augustus returned to Rome, it was to find his granddaughter ill from a fever in her wound. Her grim-faced husband presented a list of her transgressions, the greatest of which was that as she fell unconscious on the sand, her clothes torn and bloodied by the griffin, she had allowed her breasts to be glimpsed by more than a hundred soldiers.

Weeks later, after Julilla recovered, she was informed of her divorce and exiled to an island half the size of the one chosen for her mother. Without the weaving skills of the elder Julia, she went to her island in human form.

The poet Ovid foolishly earned his own exile by composing a poem about the event, all copies of which were subsequently destroyed. Yet another piece of our family's history lost forever because a woman failed to meet the standards of an antique fairytale. Apparently his description of Julilla's breasts was particularly splendid.

Harpy

My mother Agrippina was a fine woman, with the diplomatic skills of the elder Julia, the military prowess of her father Agrippa and the maternal skills of a she-bear. While assisting her husband Germanicus with military campaign after military campaign, she bore six children and did her best to keep us far from Rome and the long arm of the Emperor Augustus.

My brothers were loved by the legions, who saw them as good luck charms. Caligula in particular earned his nickname 'Little Boots' for wearing a replica of their official uniform, and was utterly spoiled by the fact that there was not a Roman soldier alive who would not smile at him.

Agrippina had learned from the fates of her mother and sister. Far from the mores and restrictions of city life, she insisted that all of her children receive military training. The boys were older, and more easily assimilated into traditional methods of fighting, marching and self-defence. But Agrippina never forgot that her daughters were Julias.

By the time I was three, I was accustomed to running races and had already been taught the rudimentary methods for using a slingshot and a wooden blade. My sister Drusilla, a year younger, was particularly good at target practice, and the two of us would spend hours hurling sticks and stones to strike a sapling, counting with glee how many hits in a row we could collect.

At four, after I saved my brother from the basilisk, I was allowed a knife of my own—a proper little dagger that I kept in my boot. I hated that knife for years later, and could not help thinking that if it had been longer, or sharper, or if I had earned it just a few months earlier and been more diligent with practice in its use, I might have managed to kill the harpies that took my father's life.

You may have noticed that my family was particularly beset by curious beasts. We had also become aware of this. My mother could not ignore how many of Augustus' heirs had mysteriously died thanks to poisoned bites or wounds inflicted upon them by all manner of magical creatures. She, of course, blamed Livia.

My father Germanicus thought my mother was imagining things. But then, he was himself a grandson of Livia and intended to be Emperor someday. He did not doubt his grandmother's magic, but refused to believe that she could actually bring a curse upon the less favoured members of her own family.

The basilisk arrived less than a month after Germanicus had written a letter to Livia, politely refusing her request for him and his family to return to Rome. Another month after the basilisk, the harpies attacked.

There were a dozen of them; shrieking harridans with the wings and feet of birds, descending from the sky in gusts of wind so cold they stole our breaths away, leaving only a foul odour behind.

I clutched the baby, and Drusilla clutched me, and we stood there stupidly together in a clump. Caligula was supposed to look after us, but his attention was fixed upon the awful battle, upon the bleeding peck marks that blazed on the skin of the soldiers and our brothers. He was smiling, his eyes bright, and even at the age of four, I knew there was something terribly wrong with him.

It was my father who snatched up my sisters and me, all three of us in a clump, and carried us away from the horrible scene to hide behind the tents. He was so strong. I remember, even now, how safe I felt in his arms.

'Stay down,' he commanded, licks of blood streaking his cheeks. 'Keep the others hidden, Nilla. No matter what happens.'

That was me. Nilla, short for Agrippinilla, little Agrippina. He was the only one who called me that.

The tent-cloths stank, hot and clinging around us, or maybe it was the breaths of the harpies that we could smell. I cried a little, I think, though I was cross when Drusilla asked if that was what I was doing. I was the oldest girl, and more than that. I was a Julia. Julias don't cry. They fight.

The baby did not know she was a Julia, and she didn't

like the smell at all. She cried and cried. The tent-cloth was ripped from us, and two harpies loomed in, shedding feathers and rotted skin in all directions.

'Pretty, tasty,' lisped one.

I stabbed blindly, trying to stick one of their feet with my small knife, but it broke, and that was the end of that. So much for being a Julia.

Blood fountained over us all as my father beheaded both creatures with a swipe of his sword. A claw burst through his body. He swayed for a moment, and then fell. There was nothing we could do to stop the other harpies leaping upon his body, and tearing him apart.

We survived. The rest of us all survived. And we never forgot.

After that we returned to Rome, and joined the household of my grandfather's wife. Livia. Bitch of Rome. My mother never again voiced her belief that Livia was responsible for the misfortunes of our family, not in front of the children. But we knew her thoughts.

Lamia

You may have heard of the lamia, a host of serpentine women who drink the blood of children. They are seductive creatures as well, taking lovers purely to keep themselves fuelled with heat and blood.

Part serpent, part bird, all monster.

I trust you have also heard the rumours that my great-grandfather's wife Livia was one of them, a poisonous creature who swept the world of anyone she saw as a rival to herself, or to her son. Those rumours are true.

Julia Agrippina's Secret Family Bestiary

I have dissembled with my previous descriptions of Livia only in refusing to acknowledge that I come from her bloodline as well as that of Augustus. On my mother's side, I am descended directly from the first Emperor, but on my father's ... ah, yes. My father Germanicus was the son of Drusus, beloved younger brother of Tiberius, both sons of the woman who ruled us all for so very long.

Livia separated the world into those who were of use to her, and those who were expendable. She had a particular hatred for Julias. How could she not, when we had a power she could never understand, a strength that meant something beyond death to your enemies, and poison in a cup?

She was young and married, pregnant for the second time, when Augustus set eyes on her, and it is said that she so bewitched him that he had to possess her before she had even produced the baby and secured her divorce. None of the rules of society applied to Livia. Though her first husband lived, she and Augustus raised her sons in the imperial household. She was thought of as a mystic, claiming great signs from the gods in support of her new husband, and went around in the get-up of a priestess.

When Augustus' heirs started dying, no one said a word. They did not dare challenge the most powerful woman in Rome.

Julia Major fell because it was Livia who decreed she should not be forgiven, and Julilla also. Julia's boys died, one by one, and even my own father Germanicus was not safe once he had rebelled against her control. I blame Livia for all of their deaths, and I am not the only one.

'Be kind to Livia,' my mother told us when we returned

to Rome, fatherless and broken. 'Be good to Livia. Above all else, be useful to Livia, and we may live.'

Caligula was the best at it. He had a talent for charming old ladies, and put it to great effect. Livia warmed to his pretty face and eloquent tongue, and allowed him into her inner circle. He would often bring his sisters along, provided we dressed nicely and smiled sufficiently. My tongue was the sharpest and most easily given to sarcasm, and Julia Livilla was too young to properly guard herself, so Drusilla became his favourite partner in crime.

More than once, when Caligula had visited our great-grandmother alone, I saw marks on his neck that might have been bites. Livia was always rosier of cheek and more pleasant company after one of those visits.

Drusus and Nero, our older brothers, were often called in for such conferences themselves, and afterwards seemed sluggish and dull. Caligula, though, thrived on Livia's attentions, and would come away from her feverish and excitable. Whatever my brother could have been; she changed him. If there is lamia blood in all of our veins, then it was brightest in his, and I believe it was her proximity that brought it out in him.

I was only alone with Livia once, the day she told me that she had arranged my marriage. I was thirteen, and old enough, so they all said. I saw a silvery sheen to the old woman's skin, and a gleam in her eyes that she was usually better at hiding. 'Are you pleased at this news?' she asked, as if I should clap my hands with joy that a fat and elderly senator had been sufficiently bribed with the gift of an imperial wife.

Julia Agrippina's Secret Family Bestiary

'Of course, grandmother,' I told her.

'Marriage is the purpose of a woman, Agrippinilla.'

I nodded and smiled, keeping my distance from her.

'Come, kiss me then.'

I froze for only an instant, horrified at the thought, then recovered myself and came forward to give her a dutiful peck on the cheek. She felt fevered, and turned her head at the last moment to receive my kiss on the mouth. I could smell warm blood, and wondered which of my brothers she had been feeding on.

'Your sons will serve me,' she breathed.

'My sons will serve the Empire,' I agreed.

She nodded and smiled, as if she had not noticed the distinction I made. 'I have made Tiberius promise,' she said. 'When I die, I must be a goddess. I will sit at Augustus' right hand as his true wife. Caligula has promised me this as well, should Tiberius fail me. And you—you will teach your sons, will you not? That Livia must be a goddess?'

'Yes, grandmother,' I managed to say. Her hands were gripping me, soft, puckered skin over bone. How long did she intend to live, if my children were to have a say in the matter?

'We are all Julias together,' she said with a wavering smile. 'I shall be Diva Julia. The first Diva Julia.'

I was almost sick at the thought of it. Here she was, stinking with the blood of my brothers, claiming a name that the Senate had only allowed her after her husband's death, when she produced a paper to say Augustus had posthumously adopted her. It was a farce that she should take the only thing we had, the name of Julia, and corrupt it to her own purpose.

'Your sons will be strong,' she promised me, and I vowed to myself that my sons would stay far away from Rome until this creature was dead.

Except, of course, that we had her in our bloodline. We were all monsters, and could never escape her.

Manticore

My mother could not hold her tongue forever, but she waited until Livia was gone. Tiberius would surely be a better Emperor, she hoped, without his bitch mother's influence.

By then, of course, it was too late. Tiberius was awash in his own corruptions, and spent most of his days frolicking on Capri with a legion of boyish throats to drink from. He had no love for any of us but my brother Caligula, who used what he had learned at Livia's lap to seduce our uncle into compliance.

I often thought my brother was play-acting the part of Tiberius' devoted follower, just as he had calculated his performance for Livia. But where does the play end and real life begin, if the artifice is needed every day, every waking moment?

What is the difference between pretending to be a monster, and actually being one? I never knew how strongly the lamia blood flowed in my brother's veins, but I do know that Caligula was not the same after his years in close contact with Livia, and then Tiberius. I also know that his performance saved me and my sisters from a similar fate, though I was never sure if that was intentional on his part.

Nothing he did was going to save our brothers, or our mother. Tiberius loathed them. He resented their brute strength, their power and popularity. My mother did not have to conspire against him (though of course she did) for him to grow suspicious.

I have no doubt my mother would have assassinated Tiberius if she could have, and that she was plotting to make her move. In the end, her crime was to refuse to eat an apple from the Emperor's hand, suspecting it to be poisoned. He smiled at the insult and had her arrested. There are many ways to poison an enemy.

Once more, a Julia was exiled from Rome to an island. But Julia Agrippina and her two eldest sons were the first to be sent to an island designed to kill them. Pandataria had teeth and claws. It was the home of the manticores, dread creatures with the faces of humans, bodies of lions, and serpentine tails lashing with scorpion stings.

They do not kill you, those stings. I have seen them used in battle and as a tool for assassination. Were I not as accomplished with the blade as I am, I might have used them myself.

The manticore's sting poisons the blood first, and destroys the body. Next time you walk, it is on paws, with only your face remaining. They create more of themselves, and I can only hope there is nothing left of the mind, or I would never sleep a night without dreaming the horror of what was done to my mother, and to Nero and Drusus.

My only comfort is that our family took its revenge against Tiberius.

Naiad
From when we were young, my sisters and I loved to swim.

No matter which country we were in, no matter if the soldiers were nearby. My mother encouraged it. *If you can swim*, she told us, *you can escape.*

In Rome, we could no longer swim in the open air, but there were the baths, as large as lakes, and we honed our skills.

I swam with Drusilla and Livilla every day, even the morning after my wedding when my body was aching painfully from my introduction to a wife's duty.

When we tired of the heat and bustle of Rome in summer, we would travel to a family villa on the coast, though we women were not permitted to set foot on Tiberius' island of boy children and debauchery, as our brother was.

'Caligula will never kill him,' Drusilla sighed one day. 'He has pledged his loyalty to Tiberius.'

'We owe that man no loyalty after what he did to our mother and the boys,' I muttered.

'You know our brother,' said Livilla. 'He can't bear to give up his performance. If Uncle Tiberius sensed even a hint of disloyalty, he would kill us all in an instant.'

One of us, and later for the life of me I could not remember which, said, 'Not if we kill him first.'

We looked across the bay, all three of us, calculating whether it might be possible to swim all the way to the island.

The first time we tried, we gave up too soon, exhausted and bruised by the current. The second time, as our muscles screamed the impossibility of the task at us, the naiads came.

They were green and blue and nothing-coloured, with sharp teeth and gleaming eyes, and my first thought was that they had come to drag us under, to finish us off. But they swam beside us and under us, giving us strength, whispering with disapproval when any of us flagged.

We reached the island not long after noon, and found my uncle sleeping in the sun, surrounded by the drowsy bodies of freshly-bitten boys.

'This was our island once,' the naiads whispered.

My sisters and I were dripping and smeared with seaweed, half naiad ourselves, and we hissed along with them, drunk on our own borrowed power.

'Take it back,' we told them.

They pounced, the naiads, and we pounced with them. The taste of my uncle's blood was the sweetest thing I have ever drunk.

By the time Caligula came along the beach to find himself the new Emperor of Rome, we had slithered back into the sea, and when he came by boat to break the news to us, we had recovered our sensibilities and respectable dress.

We were the sisters of the Emperor now, after all. We had a public reputation to uphold.

I never became a naiad again, and I do not think my sisters did either, but after that day we always salted our food more heavily, and took great pleasure in swimming in the sea. That whole first year as the sisters of the Emperor, as we gloried in our new public role, fine seats in the theatre, and the restoration of honours to our dead mother, as my husband's seed finally grew a baby inside me, the greatest luxury I enjoyed was to swim in the sea, drunk on salt and heady with the whispering song of the naiads.

***

Peacock

Livia was not the first goddess of our family. Tiberius ignored his promise to her, and Caligula did likewise. For all their crimes, I cannot blame them for fearing the possibilities of Diva Livia. Even after her death, we were all afraid of her.

She was lamia, after all. Who was to say she might not come back, given the least amount of encouragement?

In any case, Caligula might have relented, as he always felt it was unlucky to break his word even to the most dangerous of relatives, but events overtook him.

The three of us were honoured with the glory usually given to the wife of an Emperor—as it should be. We were Julias, and for the first time Rome was ruled by a man who was not afraid of what that name meant.

Caligula's wives were nothing but vessels for his children, and were of little account when he had Drusilla at his side, golden and glowing. She had always been his favourite, and he named her his heir, with Livilla and I honoured as her companions. The three of us were finally able to train openly with the soldiers, and to use our strength and power in service to the Emperor. He never went anywhere without a sister to protect him.

We were draped with jewels and precious metals, but these were weapons too. Everything we owned had an edge to it. Which was important, because from the moment he became Emperor, people were trying to kill our brother.

For the first time, we had no close relatives to fear, as we were the last scions of our family (discounting stupid old Uncle Claudius, of course, who was rarely away from his books), but the curse of the Caesars continued, and magical creatures of all kinds turned against Caligula and his rule.

I and my sisters fought bears, chimaera, sphynxes, dragons and all manner of beasts sent against my brother by foreign powers, or priests who would prefer to rule the Senate without a Caesar in command.

No Emperor has ever had an honour guard as magnificent or glorious as Caligula's sisters.

It lasted such a short time. Drusilla battled griffins one day, defending Caligula while Livilla and I were attending to our babies, and she took a wound. Barely a scratch, but it went bad, and no amount of magic could touch it.

Caligula went half insane trying to save her. He wallowed in his lamia nature, trying to bite the infection out of her, to drink the poisoned blood and spit it on the floor.

She would have died, I think, no matter what, but his ministrations certainly hastened her departure.

Our beloved Drusilla, then, was the first goddess of the Julian family. Caligula gave her priests and temples, and where the Caesar gods had the eagle, Drusilla had the peacock. The city of Rome worshipped her dutifully in the hopes that their devotions would heal the Emperor's pain.

But nothing could heal Caligula, after that. He would not see or speak to me, and though Livilla managed to comfort him for a short while, he soon turned against her too. One of his wives bore a son, and he was so determined that the child be our sister reborn, we eventually helped her to swap the baby for a girl child, out of fear for what he might do to the boy.

The situation worsened, and for the sake of our families, Livilla and I left Rome, performing what imperial duties we could, at a distance. Everything we heard of Caligula, after that, was awful. His rule became a new performance, one of maniacal grief and abuse of powers. He filled the palace with peacocks, talking to them as if they were Drusilla, feeding them from his plate, bathing them with sweet oils. When his rages got the better of him, he would strangle one of the birds with his bare hands, only to blame the nearest servant and send him to execution. Our hearts broke for him, but we stayed away until we heard that he was dead.

He was the first Emperor, as far as I knew, not to die at the hands of a family member. It was the Senate and the Praetorian Guard, sick with fear for their own families, who turned against him in the end. Had I been there, or Livilla, we could have taken the rule of the city in the name of Caligula's son, or hers, or mine. Then again, perhaps we would have torn ourselves apart trying to decide which baby to elevate.

We destroyed ourselves in any case; it merely took longer.

By the time Livilla and I returned to the city with our families, daft old Uncle Claudius was on the throne. The cunning fellow had played the fool for fifty years, and the Praetorian Guard had set him on the throne thinking he would be kindly and the city might prosper with Caligula out of the way.

We knew better. That man was a grandson of Livia, and the only good person ever to come from her bloodline was our dear dead father.

The first thing Emperor Claudius did was to name Livia a goddess. She had loathed him in life, the only one of her family who was crippled and useless, and yet he was good to her in death. It was the last good thing he did, for he followed that act by closing our sister's temple, and ordering priests to slit the throats of the peacocks. I can understand that part, in a way. It must have taken months to clean the filthy rooms where they had been housed, to reclaim the palace as a place of business rather than a chaotic, stinking zoo.

Part of me, though, wanted to kill him, when I heard what he had done. Caligula's madness was infectious enough that it was like losing Drusilla all over again.

I killed Uncle Claudius eventually, of course. We take our satisfactions where we can.

Sphynx

My sister Julia Livilla killed herself, not long after the reign of Claudius began. At least, I believe she meant to do it.

No one, not even a Julia, can take on a pack of sphynxes on her own and survive.

It was rumoured that Claudius suspected her of conspiring against him: that he sent an order for her to be exiled to one of those islands that our forebears had been so fond of, and executed there by starvation. It was also rumoured that she caught wind of the order before it officially reached her, and threw herself into battle against the sphynxes to control her own destiny, and the manner of her death.

I can well believe he sent the order, and that she responded thus to the news. All the pieces make sense, except for one.

My sister could swim. The naiads would have helped her. Why did she not accept her exile and then escape?

I will never know. Once she left me, I was alone in the world but for my five-year-old son, Nero.

Triton

Years passed. I lost my first husband and acquired a second. I fell in and out of exile as my behaviour pleased or displeased my uncle. When my second husband died, I inherited enough wealth to be in comfort regardless of what pension my uncle chose to award me.

Then there was Messalina, tiresome witch that she was, my uncle's half-witted wife. Her attempts to style herself a Julia were boring at best, and dangerous at worst. She liked to dress in a fashionable mockery of the garments that my sisters and I had worn to defend our brother's body, and she played with swords and knives so spindly and delicate as to be utterly useless.

She once freed a basilisk from the imperial collection, in the hope it would attack my son, only to claim I had opened the cage door myself when three dead slaves were found as a result of her actions.

But nothing revealed her stupidity so effectively as the matter of the sea monster.

I was in favour with my uncle that summer, as was my son Nero, who was far stronger and manlier in appearance than Messalina's timid boy, Brittannicus. For my birthday, my uncle hired a troupe of mummers to enact a tale of mermaids and sirens in the moonlight, quite obviously intended to pay homage to the stories of myself and my dead sisters. It was a sweet gesture, even if it riled his wife.

Julia Agrippina's Secret Family Bestiary

In an attempt to upstage me, Messalina gathered the priestesses of Rome to perform the song of the sea, and intentionally or not, their song drew danger down upon us all.

The Triton was roused from the deeper waters. Father of the naiads, this beast was a monstrous sea daemon, eight feet tall, with the head of a man, the tail of a fish and the teeth of a shark. He and his daughters burst out of the waves, snarling and hissing. The priestesses and revellers ran, overturning jugs of wine and bowls of bread, and the guards drew in to protect the body of the Emperor.

The shock of what she had done obviously went to Messalina's head, for she was under the impression that she could do something to combat the monster. I willed for her to do so, in the hopes that the silly bitch might get her head snapped off.

Instead, as she faced down the Triton with her thin needle of a sword, he snarled a salty belch in her direction and the wretched woman fainted dead away.

'Watch, Nero,' I whispered to my son. 'Your mother is a Julia, and you must never forget what that means.'

He watched, wide-eyed, while I took a *gladius* from the nearest soldier and butchered the beast in front of him. The naiads hissed in displeasure at me as their father's blood ran black over the sand, but they withdrew and left us in peace.

'Well done, Julia Agrippina,' Uncle Claudius said diplomatically, and I bowed to the crowd. Messalina chose that moment to awake from her faint, demanding that everyone fuss over her instead of giving me my plaudits.

It was of little account. Within a year, she managed to get herself divorced and beheaded in no particular order, and Uncle Claudius had decided that his next wife had to be a Julia.

Unfortunately for me, I was the only eligible candidate.

Vampires

The difference between a lamia and a vampire is a subtle one, and not easily divided between the female and the male. Livia was all lamia, and took her strength from feeding upon the blood of young men. Tiberius was the same. Others in our family only had a touch of the lamia about them—a silvery sheen to their golden hair, a gleam of silver in their blue eyes, or an otherworldly strength that could come out in times of danger.

Caligula had pretended to embrace his lamia nature, and at other times had fought it. In the end, I believe that is what consumed him, along with grief and madness. He was never certain whether he preferred to be predator or food.

Uncle Claudius was of a different breed. He had Livia's silver eyes, but none of the cold-blooded passions of Tiberius or Caligula. There was nothing serpentine about him. I think he was a throwback to an older creature, from before the lamia got her name.

Vampire is as good a word as any.

He was crippled, they say, from birth, which is part of the reason why Livia and the others ignored him in the tug-of-war for the succession. He limped, it is true, from a malformed leg, and his tongue stuttered when he was nervous. He preferred to spend all his time at study, locked away in his rooms and burning candles late into the night,

Julia Agrippina's Secret Family Bestiary

and it is perhaps for that reason that no one noticed that he never emerged during the day.

Had my brother Caligula been attacked at night, Claudius might not have survived to be named Emperor. But it was daylight, and he was asleep in his underground lair, and so the conspirators missed him for a crucial few hours.

Claudius drank blood, as they all did, but his taste was for women, not boys, and he had a favourite mistress who was adept at finding new slaves to meet his needs.

Perhaps I should have swum away then, when Claudius declared he wanted to marry me. I should have escaped while I could. But the death of the Triton was a recent memory and I could not trust the naiads to support me as once they had. As well as that, there was my son, my darling Nero, and I had little confidence that his swimming stroke was as smooth as my own. I had done my best with him but he was such a clumsy boy.

Claudius' own son, Britannicus, was born of a disgraced mother, whose bloodline was obviously weak. The boy was pale like his father, and did not thrive on blood, no matter how pretty and plump the slave was. If I was clever, my own son could replace him in Claudius' heart.

So I submitted to my uncle. I gave him the golden Julia wife he wanted to show off in public. I wore my swords and knives again, and the jewelled costumes that had so pleased Caligula.

I gave Claudius access to my body, lying prettily on the bed as he pawed and suckled at me, his ice-cold prick barely managing to stiffen long enough to penetrate me. How had he sired a child on Messalina? He was hardly human and his fumbling attempts to play husband to my wife were, in the end, of no account.

Claudius had a daughter, from long before he came to power, and in those days had not dared to name her Julia. It was a shame for her. Julia Octavia might have had the strength to be a true partner to the Emperor Nero and the world would have been so very different.

But it was Claudia Octavia who married my son, a weak shadow of a girl who barely even showed the gleam of the lamia bloodline. She was an excuse for my son—now Claudius' by adoption—to become the first heir of the empire, over and above Brittannicus.

Every day, I saw Claudius falter. He never could make up his mind to anything without laborious footnotes to support each decision. I began to see that look in Octavia's eyes, the same hatred Livia had once turned upon my mother, and I knew I could not trust her to be true to my Nero.

If only he could have kept from hitting her, just for a year or two.

Claudius had to go, before he had a chance to take back the honours he had allowed us, and it would be pretty perhaps to tell you a tale that would make me look more sympathetic. Perhaps I could not stand my uncle-husband's cold, clammy vampire body touching mine. Perhaps he taunted me about the death of my brother or my sisters, and I snapped. Perhaps he caught me with one of the daylight lovers who sometimes warmed my bed, and threatened me with an island, or a beheading, as I covered my body with shame and fear.

Or, perhaps, I entered the chamber where he liked to sleep away the daylight hours, deep in the bowels of the palace, his arms crossed neatly over his chest. Perhaps I thrust a sharpened stake into his heart, giving him no chance to defend himself.

He had killed so many. He was as much a monster as every other Emperor our family had created. Was it so wrong?

Nero became the next Emperor. He was older than Britannicus, and had the demure Octavia at his side. He was the son of the last living Julia. It was a popular choice. But there was Britannicus, pale and spindly, and undeniably still alive. He showed no sign of conspiring against us, and yet he lived as a reminder of how we had reached this place. His very existence was a threat.

I poisoned Britannicus. I will admit to that. Not mushrooms, nor any of Livia's old tricks. I did not even call creatures down upon him to allow myself to blame the family curse.

I poisoned him with words. I had done so from the moment I joined their household, years earlier. Every time I had a chance to be alone with the boy, I used a kind stepmother's voice to play upon his own self-loathing. He was not as ready to forgive himself for his vampire nature as his father had been, and he was smarter than his mother. Indeed that was his curse, for he knew what it did to the slaves who were brought before him as food. He had worked out easily enough how they were disposed of, once their blood no longer tasted sweet enough.

Britannicus hated himself more with every draught he took, and I had been working on him for seven long years before he broke, finally, a year into Nero's reign, and starved himself into the grave.

I no longer recognised myself. My mother would have turned her face from me in shame. But my son, I had only my son, and his future.

My son was Caesar, Emperor of Rome. He was safe.

If only the women who loved him had been safe from him.

Werewolves

It is a hard thing, to be married to a werewolf. Their bodies are unnaturally strong, and they thrive on rough play. They require far more sex than a normal husband and they leave bruises.

The first Julia learned this, when she was married to Agrippa, but it was her blessing that she had a fierce sexual appetite, and matched him, body for body. It is no wonder that rumours of her adulterous behaviour did not begin until long after he was dead. The wolf kept her well satisfied, and her later husbands did not.

The werewolf strain did not breed true through our family line. There is something odd about the combination with lamia, I think, which kept it at bay. Julia's children, including my mother Agrippina, were strong and stocky, as I have mentioned, and had something of the wolf's raw power about them, but they were not subject to the moon or the shapeshifting, as Agrippa had been.

My mother had to depilate more often than most women—she required two extra body slaves to deal with this matter alone—but I am almost certain she never bayed at the moon.

I and my sisters owed nothing to the wolf, I was sure of that. We were strong, and powerful, and beautiful. We drew

Julia Agrippina's Secret Family Bestiary

swords and bows faster than any man, ran faster, swam harder, but that was because we were Julias, and destined for greatness. It was not Agrippa's blood that made us special, it was our own.

My elder brothers may have had a little wolf in them. I am sure that is why Tiberius disliked them so much, just as the lack of wolf in Caligula's blood made him the favourite.

I had half forgotten this side to my family, so busy was I keeping an eye on the lamia amongst us, until my first husband was chosen for me.

Domitius was a distant cousin, and it became clear quite quickly that he was of Agrippa's ilk. Sadly, he had never trained as a soldier and had none of my grandfather Agrippa's restraint. He was quick to anger and would take it out on me in the bedroom.

Like the first Julia, I was a hot-blooded woman, but it was not my husband who taught me my passions. With him, I would grit my teeth and wait for it to be over. It was worst near the full moon when he would fly into rages, pin me to walls, and hurl my favourite furniture until I had nothing precious left to me.

I learned to manage him. Such is a wife's duty, and it is not difficult if she is intelligent and resourceful. I found slave girls for him to burn out his anger on before he even reached my bed. I arranged for him to play gladiatorial games with other senators, and sometimes amused myself by laying successful bets on the outcome of the matches.

I bought slaves for myself, as well. Lovely maidens with talented fingers and tongues. Glistening, oiled athletes whom I allowed to penetrate me on the days I could not fall pregnant.

All my training and battle-readiness in the service of my brother allowed me to defend myself against my husband, and once I started wearing my gilded blades around the house, he stopped trying to throw me into walls.

Perhaps, you think, knowing all this, I should have had more sympathy for my son's wife Octavia, when he began to beat her. I did not. By that time, I was a different woman. I was not the powerful young Julia Agrippina who had two sisters at her side and the world at her feet. I was a marble statue, a woman with nothing left to lose but the love of her son.

Oh, Nero loved me. I made sure of that. He had no respect for Octavia, lesser breed of woman that she was. I was the august lady who appeared on my son's coins, and sat at his side in the triumphs. When Nero named old dead Claudius a god, it was I who wore the robes of priestess and built temples in my former husband's honour.

Octavia faded into my shadow, invisible and useless. She was not even clever enough to bear a child, the one thing I could not do for my son.

Meanwhile, I knew well how to handle a man who followed the moon. I provided earthy, unmarriageable mistresses to serve my son's appetites, and ensured he had plenty of space to run and fight and howl one week out of every month. I curbed his more ridiculous expenses and kept the Senate happy enough with his imperial decisions.

Poppaea, though. Poppaea slipped by me, wretched minx: while I was distracted by the demands of government, my son started fucking a wench I had not approved.

Her influence was hardly noteworthy at first, but my son's

Julia Agrippina's Secret Family Bestiary

other mistresses began to fall away, or die of mysterious complaints. I was busy scanning the horizon for the type of magical creatures who attack our family when we least expect it, and meanwhile, Nero's new human girlfriend was slumming it with everyday poisons.

Crude, but effective.

I first noticed Poppaea's influence when she had Octavia shipped off to Pandateria, the isle of manticores. Nero had passed the order through Senate while I was in a meeting with foreign dignitaries, and I was horrified to hear of it after the fact. Octavia was of no real value to me, but the people still believed theirs had been a love match, and this would harm my son's popularity.

Besides, of all the islands he could choose, why that one? Deliberate cruelty on his part to mimic the death of my mother? More likely, it was Poppaea who sought to wound me indirectly, with a manticore's sting.

I tried to save Octavia, but for once my son's ears were closed to me, and I lost the argument. In fury, I withdrew my support for his government, leaving him to stumble through the bureaucracy without my advice and hard work, and he lashed out in kind, accusing me of all manner of crimes.

My son is a half-rate Emperor, but when he bites, he takes the whole hand.

I retired to the country, bowing out with as much grace as I could muster. Let him see how hard it is to rule the Empire without his mother cleaning up all his mistakes.

The first assassin, I blamed on Poppaea. But they came with startling regularity after that, armed with knives and swords and bludgeoning weapons. One delivered a bed designed to collapse on me, which was easy enough to evade. But I have lost three slaves to poison-tasting over the summer, and it is getting harder to convince myself that it is all her, that the wench who stole my son is solely responsible for the men who try to take my life.

Am I so much of a threat to him? Does he really believe that I would harm him? Everything I have done was for him: for his power base, his safety, his future.

I nursed a werewolf at my breast, and let him thrive. Now I have set him loose upon the world. This is my legacy: the son who sits in Rome, and the scrolls I have filled with my words over the last several months.

This, then, is the history of our family: of Caesars and Julias, monsters and murderers. I want to go back and ink over the ugly parts, leaving only the lines that express how beautiful we were, how mighty and strong and loving.

There are days when I want to burn every word.

My long, cold war with my son has come to an end. He writes that he has forgiven me my transgressions, and that he hopes I will forgive him likewise. He writes that Poppaea is gone, that he should never have chosen the lying bitch over his beloved, loyal mother. He writes that blood is the most important bond we shall ever have.

I want to believe that it is true, but it is a full moon tonight, and can I really believe that he has chosen this day, this week, this month to act with civility?

Nero has sent a ship. It floats in the bay, waiting for me. A splendid vessel, decorated in gold and pearls, the deck strewn with flowers and garlands. My son begs me to sail to Rome,

Julia Agrippina's Secret Family Bestiary

to greet him publicly and show the citizens that our enmity is over. We can begin again.

What choice have I, but to forgive and accept forgiveness? I am a Julia, and we were born to serve and protect the Emperors of Rome.

I am the last of my breed.

Tomorrow, I will stand upon the prow of that boat and bid the sailors take me to my son. If this is my fate, I will follow it. If this is a gift, I will accept it with love and gratitude. If this is a trap, let it be sprung.

If my son has betrayed me, and the ship fails, then...

I am a Julia. I can swim, and I am strong. I will make for the shore.

Lamia Victoriana

The poet's sister has teeth as white as new lace. When she speaks, which is rarely, I feel a shiver down my skin.

I am not here for this. I am here to persuade my own sister, Mary, that she has made a terrible mistake, that eloping as she has with this poet who cannot marry her, will not only be her own ruin, but that of our family.

My tongue stumbles on the words, and every indignant speech I practised on my way here has melted to nothing. The poet looks at me with his calm, beautiful eyes, and Mary sits scandalously close to him, determined to continue in her path of debauchery and wickedness. I cannot take my eyes off the poet's sister.

She is pale all over, silver like moonlight. The pale twigged lawn of her day dress makes her skin milky and soft. I have never seen such a creature as her.

'If you are so worried about my reputation, Fanny, then come with us,' urges Mary. 'Be my companion. I know you have always longed to see the continent. We are to Paris, and later, Florence.' Her deflowering has rendered her more confident than I have ever seen her. She glows with happiness and self-satisfaction.

'You may have relinquished society's good opinion, but I cannot countenance such a thought,' I say.

But the poet's sister arches her neck and says, 'Come,' and I am lost.

Love and Romanpunk   *Tansy Rayner Roberts*

***

Within a week, it becomes obvious that they are not human. The poet and his sister enter rooms so silently, it is as if their footsteps are swallowed by the very air. When we leave hotels, one of them speaks softly to the owner, and we leave without money or promissory notes changing hands.

Language is their coin, and they buy every trinket with a pearl from their tongues. I wonder, is someone somewhere keeping track of the cost of this life of ours?

Mary is immersed in her poet. At meal-times, she gazes fiercely at his hands, as if the way that his fingers toy with the silverware or hold a wine glass are in themselves a great work of art. She sighs about hunger or thirst, but does little to assuage such desires.

I eat, but the food tastes like ashes, such is my fear. I should not have followed my sister. Her fate should not be my own. I tell myself I chose this path because of my terror of what Father would do to me if I returned without Mary, but the truth is, I came with them because the poet's sister asked me to.

On the ninth day, she kisses me.

I am distracted by my latest letter from home. The paper is clutched tightly in my fist and my first concern is passing by the poet's sister in the passageway without our skirts getting tangled together or my hip pressing unduly against hers. Unexpectedly, she turns to me so that our bodies are aligned in that narrow space and gasps her mouth against my own.

Lamia Victoriana

I drink her in for a moment of perfumed air and warmth, and then she is gone, her laughter spilling against the walls as she moves, so fast, so fast.

Gone.

Mary cups her hands over the slight swell of her belly, admiring her new curves in the mirror. 'I am greater than I was, Fanny,' she tells me. 'The world is greater than it was.'

'You are foolish in love,' I tell her, snipping off the end of my embroidery thread. Love. Is that the fluttering feeling in my bones when the poet's sister looks at me? Am I a greater fool than my sister?

'Admit it,' says Mary, tugging the silk of her dress out so that she can imagine how she will look when she is more months round. 'Paris is beautiful.'

Paris. Paris is chocolate and pastries that we do not drink or eat, though it sits prettily before us at meal-times, in perfect china vessels. Paris is expensive frocks that my sister and her poet cannot afford, persuaded from fancy shops with quiet, forceful words.

Mary buys me a travelling dress of sturdy linen and wool, with a jaunty hat. The colours are violet and black, as is proper for a widow rather than an unmarried chaperone. I wonder whom it is that I am supposed to be mourning, but I rather like the way that I look in the costume.

On the train to Florence, I stand at the window, gazing at the winding ribbon of Italian countryside. This, this is the world. I am free of the dust and the smallness of Father's house and our street in London. I feel as if I could fly.

The poet's sister brushes against me in the narrow cabin, and then again, so that I can tell it was not done by accident. Her fingertips linger on my waist as she steadies herself against the bunk. 'Shall we join Mary and my brother in the dining carriage?' she asks.

I shake my head, not willing to say aloud that I cannot bear another meal of artifice and elegance at which nothing is eaten. They all enjoy the ritual, but it only serves to remind me of what we have lost and what we have left behind. It unsettles me that such a vital human need has been lost to us.

Hungry. I am so very hungry, and yet I cannot swallow even a crumb.

'Well then,' she says, and tugs down the stiff blind that shuts out the light. 'We are alone.'

The travelling dress comes apart so easily, as if it were designed for this. A button, a lace, and I am unpeeled. Her hands are cold against the heat of my skin, and her mouth fits against my neck perfectly.

My mind is overwhelmed with her fingers, her palms, the soft mound beneath her thumb, and the whisper of my chemise as it gives way to her. I do not notice the bite until she is so deep inside me that there is no return, no escape, just heat and taste and the rocking pulse of the train through every inch of my skin.

For the first time in days, in weeks, I am sated. Finally, I understand what I was hungering for.

To be food.

***

Lamia Victoriana

Later, much later, there is a whistle. The train has stopped. I am lying dizzy in the lower bunk, my body wrapped in the languid arms of the poet's sister.

'We're here,' she says, and slides over my inert body to dress herself. I watch as her white skin disappears into layers of fabric, of stockings and stays and damask. When she is her outer self again, she turns her attentions to me, drawing me to my feet and dressing me as if I am a doll. She even combs my hair, playing the lady's maid.

When I speak, it is only to say, 'So quiet.' Where is the bustle of the other passengers, the calls and urgent conversations, the mutterings as they embark or depart?

'All the time in the world,' she says softly, and powders my face.

Every apartment on the train is empty as we pass. But no, not empty. If I look too closely, I can see a hand here, a foot there, a fallen lock of hair.

She catches me looking. 'My brother was hungry,' is her only explanation.

We meet Mary and the poet on the platform. They are bright with colour, delighted with themselves. Several porters come forth to carry our trunks, but they all have a dazed look about their eyes that proves the poet has already paid them with his dulcet words.

'I know we shall love it here in Florence,' says Mary.

'It is a most accommodating city,' agrees the poet, with a satisfied smile.

We have been in Florence only three days when someone tries to kill us. He is a most unassuming looking gentleman. The poet's sister and I are wandering the city markets, choosing furnishings and flowers that will look splendid in the new house that her brother is buying for us. He spends his days going from place to place, searching for the perfect villa, while Mary plans the garden where her children will play.

The assassin lunges out of the shadows, a rope knotted in his hands, and wraps it around my lover's throat. She is caught unawares, but he does not expect me to savage him with the fine brass door-knocker I had been admiring on a nearby stall.

Blood pours from the wound on his head as I hurl the knotted rope away, cooing over the ugly bruises it has left upon her.

'Do not concern yourself, Fanny,' she says in a beautiful rasp. 'No one shall destroy us.'

'You are not one of them,' the man gasps, holding his sleeve to the wound. 'Do not let the lamia take your will and your life from you, Frances Wollstonecraft.'

I shiver that he knows my name. Or perhaps it is that other word—lamia. I do not know what it means.

'Come near us again,' said the poet's sister, 'and my brother will kill you.' She takes my hand, and we run away together, through the market.

'Who is that man?' I ask at the supper table that night. The poet, his sister and Mary all look at each other as if I have said something unpleasant, a truth not to be named aloud. 'Why does he hate us?' I persist. Am I the only one not to know the secrets of this new family we have formed? I am not a child!

Lamia Victoriana

'He is an old enemy of my kind,' the poet says finally, shifting his wine glass one precise inch to the left, so that the candlelight makes a prettier pattern of ruby shapes on the tablecloth. 'He hates us for being. That is all. His name is Julius. He is not important.'

'He was so strong.' I can still remember that look in his eyes, as if my lady were some kind of monster.

'We are stronger,' says the poet's sister, and squeezes my fingers with her own.

From Florence, we travel to Switzerland, determined that our plan to live together in all happiness and beauty shall not be spoiled by the horrid man, Julius.

I wonder sometimes if he was sent by our father, if the poet only wished to spare Mary and I from that awful truth, that our own family would rather see us dead than happy.

We have our house of dreams, finally, in the midst of such green splendour, and a good distance outside the town where prying eyes might seek to spoil our circle. The poet and Mary visit the town often, to buy pretty trinkets, and to slake their thirst. When they are gone, it is as if the house is ours, only ours, and the poet's sister and I can finally love each other as we long to.

She needs no drink but what she takes from me in sweet drugging kisses that make me feel alive.

Mary's child is born; a perfect silver nub of a creature with bright eyes. She is hungry, so very hungry, and nuzzles her constantly, sucking, biting, clawing at her for food. She hires a nursemaid from the town, and then another, but the babe's thirst is too great, and for a while it is as if we are constantly digging graves for the scraps left behind.

Left unsaid is our belief she will not survive.

We will have to move again, and soon, but we have been so happy here. It pains us to speak of leaving the garden, the egg-shell drawing room, the balcony that looks out over the valley.

We stay too long.

I am woken from a deep befogged sleep against the body of my beloved when I hear a scream in the night. The baby makes so much noise that I am content at first to ignore the interruption, but then there is another and the shattering of glass.

The poet's sister sits up in bed, shining and glorious in her white nightgown. 'Him,' is all she says, and then she is up on her feet, hair streaming behind her, teeth gleaming in the darkness.

He has come for us.

The downstairs parlour is alight as we come down the stairs: flames crackle up the curtains and blacken the wooden walls. My beloved gasps as she finds the body of her brother in a pool of silver blood, his body pierced through the heart and his head lying some distance from his neck.

'Fanny!' Mary screams, and bursts through the flaming doorway like an angel, bearing her child wrapped in a sage-green blanket trimmed with ivory lace. 'Take her,' she begs, placing the wailing bundle in my arms.

I stand there, immobile, as Mary and my beloved turn back to the smoke and the flames, ready to avenge the death of the poet.

Lamia Victoriana

He—Julius, slayer of lamia—walks through the wall of flames with his sword held high.

It is a short sword, and bronzed rather than steel. How odd, the things you notice at such moments.

My sister bares her teeth, as sharp as those of my beloved, and they swarm him. I do not want to watch. I flee through the kitchen, where I grab the only weapon I can find, a kitchen knife, and spare cloths for the baby. Then I run out of the beautiful house, my niece crying in my arms, down the hill and away.

I feel it minutes later, the death of my beloved. It is a blossoming pain in my chest, as if someone has carved out my heart. I do not feel Mary die; we have no such connection. But my tears fall for them both.

I run and hide, but the baby is hungry and she will not stop crying. Finally I press her mouth again my upper arm and she suckles deeply, her own teeth finding the vein and drinking in great gulping swallows. I shall have to wind her afterwards, and the thought is almost enough to make me burst with laughter.

Too late. I should have silenced her minutes ago. He is upon us. I hear him treading the crisp grass nearby, and the rasp of his smoke-filled lungs. 'Frances,' he says, as if he still thinks he has an ally in me. 'Give me the child.'

The baby's feed is not as delicious as that of my beloved. It hurts, though there is still a satisfaction in it, in knowing that I am food, that I am needed. Little Mary. Mine now. 'No,' I say, quite calmly, though he is standing not far from me, and he has a sword. I do not think he will hurt me. For some reason, he does not believe I am one of the monsters.

I keep the knife hidden in my skirts so that he shall not see that I am able to defend myself.

'Listen to me, Frances. I have tracked these creatures for years. They were the last, the three up there in the house.'

My family. Tears rush anew down my cheeks and I cannot wipe them away without disturbing the babe.

'There is only that one,' he continues. 'When it is gone, the world will be safe. One less monster to ravage families, to destroy the lives of innocents such as yourself. Lamia who are born rather than made are the most powerful, the most dangerous. I have worked for centuries to weaken these creatures, and if this one lives to make more of its kind, it may be centuries more before they are wiped from the face of the earth.'

The baby releases me with a gasp and leans against my breast, breathing deeply. She is asleep. My niece, the perfect silver child. My daughter, now. He cannot even acknowledge that she is a 'she'.

'No,' I say again.

'You can go home, Frances,' he says, in a soothing voice. 'Home to your father, to your old life…'

The thought of it makes me shudder. 'No!' I scream, and run at him with the knife.

He does not expect it, even now. He thinks I am food, a docile milk cow, with no reason to defy him now that my lover and sister are dead. I catch him in the neck, and he twists badly, falling down the hillside onto his sword.

I do not think he survived. How could he, a blow like that? After months of standing aside, as my sister and the poet killed for food, I have become a murderer myself.

Perhaps the murderer of thousands, by keeping my little Mary alive. The blood of my body will not sustain her forever. But I have learned that the lamia power of persuasive words is mine to share, if I hold the baby close to my skin, and that has been enough to get us from train to train, from country to country.

We will travel as far as we can, to a land so distant that another Julius can never find us. She will grow, my darling daughter, and she will feed. Some day, perhaps, she shall make me another lover to replace what I lost. We shall be a family, all together.

She shall live, my little Mary, long after I have gone, and live, and live.

I am not sorry for it.

The Patrician

I

Clea Majora walked through the hot streets of Nova Ostia, her sandal-shod feet lightly treading on the wide, baked, paving stones. She bought a honey cake from a pastry stall and nibbled it as she walked, using the vine leaf wrapper to catch the crumbs. At the wall, a couple of boys she knew from school were playing a covert game of soccer, and called for her to join them, but she waved and kept walking. It was too hot for games, and besides, she had her own plans for how to spend the lunch hour.

Outside the stifling confines of the city, she kept walking until she came to her favourite gum tree. She unpinned her stola so that it folded underneath her when she sat down on the rough ground, and slid in the earbuds of her iPod. For a blissful forty minutes, she listened to music and a podcast about movies she would never get to see. The rest of the world existed, out there, and she liked the reminder of that.

Clea did not see the stranger until he was almost on top of her. She was startled when he tripped on a root nearby and stared at her as she yanked out her earbuds.

'I'm sorry!' he exclaimed.

'No, I'm sorry!' Quickly, Clea fastened her stola back up so that it covered the front of the *Gladiators Do It In the Arena* t-shirt she had borrowed from her brother that morning. 'I'm not supposed to be here,' she confessed. 'Not during daylight. Are you a tourist?'

'Yes,' said the stranger in a cultivated, I-was-not-born-speaking-English kind of accent. 'I suppose that I am. Are we near Nova Ostia? I lost my way.'

Tourists always came to the city by train or by coach, but were asked to walk the ten minute hike up the sloped road so that they entered the city without the ease of modern transport. Clea recognised the factory-produced tourist toga and tunic as one from Roman Road Tours. This man must have wandered away from his group. 'You shouldn't wander off-road,' she said accusingly. 'This is Australia, the bush can be dangerous.' She should tell him about drop bears. That would serve him right. She was resentful of losing the last fifteen minutes of her lunch hour. 'Come on, I'll take you.'

He wore a hat, at least. Many tourists refused, wanting the full 'authenticity' of the Roman experience, only to appear at the city gates bright red like crayfish. The city was built with shaded streets to keep the Australian sun away from bare arms and bald pates, but that ten minute walk could do a lot of damage.

The visitor wore a broad-brimmed woven straw hat, not a design Clea recognised from Roman Road Tours. His hands were blistered from their moments in the sun, but the rest of him was a paler, European colour.

Clea dropped into the usual tourist spiel, about how a replica Roman city had come to be built in New South Wales, though it wasn't really a replica, but a combination of several Roman towns. She added the part about real stone

The Patrician

from Ostia and Herculaneum having been shipped over as part of the building process.

'Yes,' said the visitor with a sigh. 'I wish you hadn't done that.'

Still, he seemed interested enough, and stopped to peer at the triumphal arch which served as the city's gateway. The soccer boys were gone, probably yelled at by one of the merchants. The worst crime in Nova Ostia was to be inauthentic where the punters might see.

'Would you like to wait for your tour group?' Clea asked politely. 'Or some refreshment, perhaps?' She would be late getting back to the thermopolium at this rate, and it would look better if she brought a customer with her.

The stranger's eyes were fixed upon the wall of the Temple of Vesta, and it was as if he had already forgotten she existed. 'Thank you,' he said absently. 'But I travel alone.'

Clea dreamed of snakes, of women with bright silver eyes. She awoke to a flickering light outside her window, which was all wrong. It wasn't like Nova Ostia had street lights. She knew even before she made it out of bed that there had to be a fire somewhere.

The Temple of Vesta was aflame. The white marble walls had turned black, at the heart of the blaze. Clea watched as various citizens ran to help, rolling out emergency hoses that had been carefully hidden in gutters and hatches. There was shouting, and urgency, and the acrid taste of smoke in the back of her throat.

A man leaped out of the flames and ran across the roof. As Clea watched, he jumped from wall to roof again, and ran along gutters, holding something the size and shape of a Roman short sword. She knew him, from his height and gait. The visitor.

Not quite knowing why, she opened her window and leaned out. He turned, his head flicking once in her direction, and then leaped—this time, arcing over the nearest wall, and vanishing from her sight.

Obviously this was the sort of thing you mentioned to people. But when the Governor's secretary went from house to house the next day, searching for any witness reports concerning the fire, Clea said nothing.

At lunchtime, she bought two pastries and a flask of water, and set out to her usual spot. The visitor was leaning against her tree, looking exhausted, his hat casting a short shadow around him like an anti-halo.

'You did it,' she said without ceremony, passing him the water first, which he gulped down. 'Didn't you?'

'Of course I did,' he said, and then looked up at her, his eyes all shaded and mysterious. 'How many bodies?'

Clea shivered; that he could talk about 'bodies' so easily, as if he were asking about her marks at school, or the number of pastries in her basket. 'Two,' she said. That was what she had heard, from her mum, the neighbours, the soccer boys. 'There were two dead women in the temple. But no one knows who they … were.' She wanted to ask him. The question bubbled up fiercely inside her, but she held it down. Something told her if she said the wrong thing, he would just walk away. No matter how tired he was.

'Damn,' he said quietly. 'One got away.'

The Patrician

Clea felt cold inside, and now she wasn't afraid he would leave—she was afraid that he wouldn't.

The man was looking at her now, his eyes intently on her. 'How old are you?'

That was the kind of question you didn't answer, not when a tourist asked you. Clea had learned that when her curves first came in. There were always older men hanging about, eyeing her shape under the stola. But he wasn't asking like that—there was nothing pervy about him, no hint that he fancied her. He was all business.

But what kind of business? Assassin? Terrorist?

'Sixteen,' she told him, and saw the interest flick away from her again. Really? She was of age, so not relevant? How creepy was that?

'Most of you sleep outside the city walls, yes?' he went on briskly. 'Are there any children who sleep inside the walls?'

'I'm not telling you that,' she snapped. 'Why should I tell you anything? This is my home, and you're—weird.' Her whole body ached to trust him, to tell him everything she knew, and that was weird too. Like she wasn't in control of her actions or her thoughts.

Something about this bloke made her throw all her sense out the window, and he was old enough to be her dad.

He nodded calmly. 'I'm sorry,' he said. 'I need information, and it's only fair I give some in return.' He paused, waiting for her to define terms.

'Who were those women?' Clea asked, her voice coming out shakier than she liked.

'Lamia,' he said, drinking another slug of the water she had brought for him. 'A kind of ancient vampire, from

Roman mythology. They seduce young men and drink their blood.'

Clea blinked. Again, he was oozing trustworthiness, like some kind of 'believe me' pheromone. It felt like the truth. 'And who are you?' she asked, changing it from 'what' only at the last moment.

'I am a traveller. The last person alive who knows what these creatures are, and how to fight them. My task is to rid the world of the beasts of Rome. When the last of them are gone, I will rest.' He sounded so casual about his death being a bullet point in the action plan.

'I meant, what's your name?' Clea asked.

He almost smiled, his face creasing under the shade of the hat. 'Julius,' he said.

'Like Caesar?'

'Yes.'

Something about him made her ask the stupidest possible question. 'You're not—actually *the* Julius Caesar?'

This time he did smile, though it looked all wrong on his face, like it wasn't an expression that happened very often. 'No. That would be somewhat bizarre.'

'There are only three families who sleep inside the walls,' she blurted out.

He switched back to the main topic without a blink. 'How many have children?'

'Ours. Just ours. My brother Ant is fourteen.' Most of the families with kids preferred to live further out, where you could have a television in the living room and didn't have to be so discreet about wifi or electric kettles.

'Excellent,' said Julius, his eyes blazing out of the shade.

The Patrician

※※※

Clea couldn't sleep. She Googled 'lamia' and came up with a few medieval bestiary wikis with less than helpful illustrations, page after page of poetry by Keats, and a few vague references to the daughters of Mary Wollstonecraft.

Julius had given her so little to go on. He had assured her that her brother was probably not in danger, that the third lamia had most likely fled the city, but Clea had not felt the pressing wave of belief that she usually did when he spoke. Perhaps he hadn't been trying so hard.

'What do I do if something happens?' she had asked.

'Call me.'

'I don't have your number. We don't have phones here! We have email, though. Do you have email?' Okay, she was babbling.

Julius shook his head as if there was something fundamental she just wasn't getting. 'If something happens, open a window and *call me*.'

Clea didn't know whether it was super mega creepy to know he would be that close by, or a complete relief. She didn't decide until morning came and her brother was still alive and annoying as ever, and she knew exactly how to feel: stupid. Ripped off. Taken for a ride. Conned.

Three days passed. Clea did her shifts in the thermopolium, idly Googled her university options, read a whole lot of manga, and almost but not quite forgot about the posh man in the straw hat.

Then one afternoon she came home to find Ant on the couch, snogging a girl. 'Ew, get a room,' she said with all the usual grace and tolerance of an older sister.

'Get a life,' muttered her brother, disentangling himself from the girl and tugging her by the hand into his bedroom. He had—ew, ew—actual love bite marks on his neck, and the girl was far too pretty and far too smug-looking, and wasn't fourteen WAY too young for that sort of thing?

Mum was going to kill Clea when she found out she had actually caused Ant to go into his room with the hot girl and close the door.

Clea tried to remember what the girl had looked like. There was a blur in her memory, like someone had reached out and smudged it with an old school blackboard duster.

Oh. Blonde hair. Silver eyes. Smug smile. Right.

Clea ran to the kitchen, threw up the window and hollered, 'JULIUS!' into the street outside. She had thirty seconds to feel idiotic about it before the door clicked and he walked in as if he owned the place.

'She's here?' he asked.

'My brother just took her into his room. For making out purposes.' She added that last part because Julius was old and might not get it if she didn't spell it out.

Julius walked swiftly ahead, and flung open the door. Clea was caught between embarrassment and curiosity as she ran after him.

Ant lay spread out on his bed, the blonde girl crouched over him, and there were more than love bites on his neck. Blood spattered the pillow, and stained the girl's mouth.

Clea hit her with a chair. It was the first thing that came to hand, and it seemed appropriate.

Julius had a sword. Where had the freaking sword come

The Patrician

from? He hacked the girl's head from her body, which took a lot more effort than in the movies, and drenched Ant's room in a silvery liquid like mercury. He then took the chair from Clea, broke a leg off it, and neatly punched it through the girl's chest.

Clea tried not to look, not to think about it, except to be glad of the silvery stuff, of the proof that things were Other in some way, that she hadn't just helped a random stranger behead her brother's first girlfriend without a really good reason. 'Will he be okay?'

Ant looked sort of dazed and blissed out, and the blood had already clotted at his neck.

Julius gave the boy a cursory look. 'She chose well. Most lamia victims drain too easily—your brother is one of the rare types who thrive on such attention. She could have fed on him for a decade, if she was careful.'

Clea shivered. 'Does that mean other lamia might come after him too? If he's an extra delicious Happy Meal?'

'Ordinarily, yes.' Julius took a small leather-bound diary from his pocket, and made a mark in it. 'But she was the last.'

Clea stared at him, stricken. 'Does that mean—you're finished? You're going to die?'

Julius gave her a brief smile. 'A pleasant thought, but no. There are many more monsters on this list. I must rid the world of all of them before I can rest.'

Clea looked around the wrecked room, at the chair and the blood-spattered bed and the body of the creature and the silvery muck sliding across the polished floorboards. 'So you do this sort of thing all the time?'

'Yes.'

'Why?'

'It is my task and my birthright,' he said simply. 'I am a Julius.'

And she wasn't mistaking that, was she, the sneaky little indefinite article that suggested Julius was not just his name, it was a Thing?

'Are you done here?' Clea asked in a small voice. 'In Nova Ostia?'

'I will help you clean up first,' Julius said, as if offended she had not taken that into account. 'Lamia blood is quite messy.'

'Yes, I'd noticed.' She wanted to keep asking questions, to get more out of him before he swanned off into the night. 'What are you?'

Julius looked pensive, as if putting it into words was something which saddened him. 'I am a manticore,' he said finally, and then sent her to fetch a bucket of soapy water and squeegees for the cleaning.

II

Ten months later, Clea went all the way with Daniel for the first time. It wasn't nearly as much fun as she had thought it was going to be, and afterwards she went to sit in her favourite spot with her back to the gum tree, listening to angsty music and feeling like her whole body could fly apart at any moment.

She didn't need to be confused any more than she already was, and she really didn't need a reappearance of Julius, not today, so of course there he was in his straw hat and his toga,

The Patrician

tripping over that same tree root, and apologising for it.

'What is it this time?' she asked, more acidly than she would have on any other day, because really, losing your virginity to a boy who had no idea what to do with it was the sort of thing that allowed you to be in a legitimate bad mood for at least a fortnight. 'Werewolves?'

Julius blinked as if she had said something quite absurd. 'Actually, the last werewolves were killed in the nineteenth century,' he said.

'You're older than you look,' Clea snarked at him. Not that she really thought he had been around killing werewolves in the nineteenth century. He couldn't be more than forty. Maybe thirty-five.

'Yes, probably,' he said. And then, 'How do you feel about gargoyles?'

That was how Clea ended up spending her whole weekend clambering around on the roofs of Nova Ostia, pointing out every animal-shaped statue on every building, and helping Julius to discreetly shatter them.

'I always wondered,' she said. 'They didn't seem a very Roman sort of thing.'

'The creatures are, the statues aren't,' he said. 'They're attracted to cities, especially the high parts, where they can see the stars. They climb up here and just ossify. Which is fine until they come to life during the full moon and start biting chunks out of people.'

'Why didn't you smash them up last time you were here?' she asked.

'They weren't here last time I was here,' he replied.

Clea argued he was wrong, that many of the gargoyles had been there since she was a child, and Julius argued that in fact memory alteration was part of their self-defence mechanism, and what with one thing and another, she completely forgot about Daniel and how weird it was to let someone inside your actual body, and how she had been wanting to explode into a million pieces.

When the last gargoyle was destroyed, Clea and Julius stretched out in the shade of the aqueduct, on the flat roof of the temple of Saturn. It was too hot to climb back down to ground level.

'Do you want to kiss me?' she asked him.

He looked surprised. 'No thank you.'

'Are you gay?' she asked next. Apparently she was going with personal questions this time round.

'No,' said Julius, still polite and friendly about the whole thing. No hint of embarrassment. 'I'm just terribly old.'

Clea lifted herself up on her elbows, staring at him. 'Did you really kill werewolves in the nineteenth century?'

'Among other things.'

Wow, okay. So not thirty-five. 'That means you were born in—eighteen hundred and something?'

'No,' Julius said calmly. 'Further back.'

'When?'

He sighed. 'Thirty-nine.'

'1739?' Australia hadn't even been colonised then. Not that she thought he was Australian. It was just—a really long time ago. Hard to take in.

'No. Just 39.'

'*A.D.?*' Clea said in a voice that was supposed to be all

The Patrician

cool but came out as sort of a shriek.

'Scholars say C.E. these days. It's important to move with the times.'

'But that makes you nearly two thousand years old!' So much older than thirty-five. Older than most *cathedrals*.

'Yes,' said Julius, looking tired. 'I suppose it does.'

'How does that even work?'

'It's a long story.'

'Obviously!' Clea thought it over for a while. The heat was making her brain slow and mushy. 'Are you the only person in the world who's all immortal and monster-hunting?'

'As far as I know.'

'So you don't have sex because we're all too young for you?'

'I didn't say that,' he said with a hint of a smile. 'But you are definitely too young for me.'

'My grandmother needs a boyfriend. I could totally hook you up.'

'Excellent, I look forward to that.' Julius sat up suddenly, looking distracted. 'We missed one.'

'We did? Where?'

And then a gargoyle came screaming over the roof at them, belching smoke, and they had more important things to worry about than a conversation about sex with old people.

III

Clea was nineteen, home on holiday from university, when she got a chance to ask Julius why the creatures he hunted came to Nova Ostia so often.

'This is three times in three years now,' she said when she found him battling naiads in the Fountain of Neptune, at four o'clock in the morning. 'Wouldn't it save time just to stay here and wait for them all to come to you?'

'And leave the rest of the world unprotected?' he said, throwing handfuls of iron shavings into the water despite the wails and cries of the blue-skinned women. 'It might seem like a regular occurrence to you, but it's merely a drop in the ocean.'

'Still, it's a weird coincidence that the ones who make it as far as Australia always come here.'

'Not a coincidence at all,' said Julius, wiping scales off his toga. 'The people who built this little tourist trap of yours used actual stone from Roman cities, remember? The creatures are drawn here just as much as they are to Ostia itself, or Pompeii, or Bath.'

'Bath in England?'

'Lots of museums in Bath. Old temples. Statues. I spend a great deal of time in museums.' He looked curiously at Clea. 'What are you studying at university?'

'Economics,' she said, which was a lie. Later, when the naiads had gurgled their death throes and she was letting Julius clean himself up in her mum's *ensuite*, she admitted, 'Archaeology and Latin.'

He seemed amused. 'I suppose there isn't a course on hunting mythological beasts.'

'Not specifically. Sydney universities are quite provincial. I was lucky to get Latin.'

Julius dried his face on a shell pink hand towel. 'You're still too young for me.'

The Patrician

'Did I ask?' Clea was pissed off that he assumed she was still interested. 'I have a boyfriend. Who is very good in bed, actually.'

'I'm glad you told me that. I might have had sleepless nights, wondering about it.'

Clea glared at him. 'Are we done here?'

'That depends on you, doesn't it?'

She could have kicked him out, shut the door, and ignored him until next time their paths crossed and there were dragons, or something, but it had been two years, and she had a whole lot more questions saved up. 'I'll walk you out.'

They strolled through the quiet city. 'Tourists still come to this place?' Julius asked. 'I didn't think anyone cared about the ancient world any more.'

'Gladiator gaming is trendy again,' said Clea. 'It helps. Though the visitors are always disappointed we don't have a Colosseum with real fighting and stuff.'

'Bread and circuses. Nothing changes.'

'Mostly we get Australians who want to travel for culture but feel guilty about their carbon footprint. Never mind that it will take another fifty years to pay back the carbon footprint it cost to build this place…'

Julius nodded. They were almost at the wall. 'What else did you want to ask me this time?'

'The first time we met, you said you were a manticore, which was a lie because I looked it up, and it's like—a lion mixed with a person and a scorpion, and unless you're very good at disguises, that's not what you are.'

Clea waited for him to tell her that yes, he was a lion and a scorpion and a person all mixed together, and his human

65

skin had been sewn by dwarves, or something.

'The manticore was a metaphor,' Julius answered instead. 'Like a chimaera, or a griffin. A creature built from other creatures. A hybrid. That's what I am.'

'But a hybrid of what?'

He shrugged. 'There is lamia blood in my family. Werewolf too. Other magics. One of my great-grandmothers turned herself into a dragon to prove a point. Many of my relatives became gods. We were a strange family.'

'And your name is really Julius?'

Clea had done her research. She wasn't limited to Google anymore; she had a whole university library at her disposal. The year 39 C.E. was during the reign of Caligula, one of the emperors who claimed descent from Julius Caesar. Then again, it wasn't only emperors who used the name. Any slave freed from that family could call himself Julius.

He sighed. 'I told you it was a long story.'

'I'm young, remember?' Clea said pointedly. 'I have time.'

Julius took her hand, an odd gesture that had nothing romantic about it, and everything to do with the fact that they were like teammates now. They had killed lamia and gargoyles and naiads together. He led her out of the city, to the tree where she had spent so many of her teen years being all angsty. He didn't trip over the tree root this time.

They made themselves comfortable, and he told her a story.

'I was born Julia Drusilla, in the year 39,' he began.

'You were born a girl?' Clea interrupted. Whatever she had expected, it was not that.

'No. I was a boy. But my father desperately wanted a

girl. He was still in mourning for his favourite sister, and he had made her a goddess. In his head, this daughter was to be her replacement, her namesake, her human form on earth. He could not comprehend that I was a boy. It's funny, really. Every other emperor obsessed about their sons and male heirs. Mine saw no need for that, as he planned to live forever.'

'Your father was Caligula,' said Clea, who had guessed that much but wanted to be certain.

Julius gave her a wary look. 'Indeed. You probably want me to defend him, to say he was nothing like the monster that appears in the history books, and that much at least is true. He was a very different monster to the one history recalls.'

'Was he a manticore too? Part lamia, part werewolf…'

'Part sociopath. Yes. More lamia than anything, but that was Livia's fault. I'm getting ahead of myself. My mother was worried for me—that if Caligula realised I was a boy, I might be in danger. She bought a baby girl—from a slave, I suppose—and swapped us over. I was safe in the temple of the Vestals when, two years later, there was a palace uprising against my father. He was killed, and my mother, and the false Julia. Uncle Claudius was made Emperor instead, and he named his daughters Claudia, not Julia. I was the last of my kind.'

'It's quite a common name these days,' Clea commented.

Julius seemed impatient with her. 'It means nothing in the mouths of anyone else. To my family, it was of great significance, to be a Julia. Just as it meant something to have lamia blood, or werewolf, or dragon. I still had two living aunts who visited me in my childhood sometimes, who trained me to use my powers. Julia Livilla made the list for me, of the creatures we had to defeat, to free our family of the curse. Julia Agrippina taught me my weapons, and took me travelling around the world. After they were gone, I fought the creatures alone.'

Clea felt a sharp twist in her stomach when he said the word 'alone'. It was only a slight hesitation, but he held himself so rigidly, as if admitting the word meant something might destroy his whole illusion.

He continued. 'Nero, my cousin, was the last Julian Emperor. He died when I was twenty-nine. It was some years before I realised I had stopped aging. It was as if … as the only member of the family who had survived, I now held all of their burdens. It took decades before I realised what my task in life was. My aunt's list. The creatures that had to be destroyed.'

'But you don't know for sure,' Clea said softly. 'That it's what you have to do. That you can … rest, when the list is complete.'

His eyes were burning now with a fierce, angry light. 'Oh, yes. I know.'

She wanted to comfort him. To reach out and touch him. To be something, anything that he needed. But she had nothing to offer—nothing that he would take, anyway.

They sat together until morning. She dozed once, leaning against his shoulder and the tree, and when she blinked awake, she was alone.

She did not see him again for five years, and when she did, he was too busy stabbing harpies to stop and chat.

The Patrician

IV

Clea grew up, and built a life. Archaeology remained her passion for fifteen years, and after that she wrote books, because there was less mud and fewer long haul flights involved, and you had to think about that carbon footprint these days.

She mostly lived in Europe. When she returned to Australia to visit her family, it was not to Nova Ostia, which had closed to the public some time around her thirtieth birthday, but to Sydney, which had rather fewer incursions of mythical creatures who wanted to kill people, and hardly any visits by the man whose job it was to destroy those creatures, on behalf of a host of dead Julias.

She saw Julius in Venice, though, and Rome, and London, more than once. Sometimes they talked, sometimes they killed things. At least once, there was nothing to talk about and nothing to kill, and so they had a nice dinner in an Indian restaurant, because they were both hungry, and it was there.

Clea had children and got married, in that order.

When she was fifty-three, she went to the opera, not because she wanted to, but because her husband had hated it with a vengeance, and she was angry at him for dying so suddenly, with no warning, of a heart attack.

Opera seemed the best revenge.

She wore a vintage gown of purple silk that hugged the curves which had spread, somewhat, over the years. She wore diamonds that had belonged to her grandmother and usually lived in a safe.

Halfway through the second act, a dragon marched

across the stage, which had not been mentioned at all in the programme. Clea did not realise she had been holding her breath until a man in an ill-fitting costume strode across the stage after the dragon, and leapt on to its back.

There was fire and screaming and the horrible ripping sound as velvet curtains were destroyed, and very little singing. But when it was over, the audience had mostly fled, and there was a dead dragon on the stage.

Clea walked on unsteady feet up the aisle, and gazed at the man who was half-draped over the dead dragon in exhaustion. 'I like the beard,' she said finally.

'It's false,' said Julius, removing it.

'I know. I like the fact that you went to so much trouble to assemble a Don Claudio costume despite the fact that the dragon was sure to send the audience packing anyway.'

'It's all about style,' he said, and let out a heavy sigh.

'You're wounded,' she said.

'I'm never wounded. Didn't you hear, I'm quite good at this.'

She leaned over and poked at the bloody hole in his chest. 'You're wounded.'

'Ouch.' He looked down in alarm. 'Damned spurs. I didn't see that coming. What do I do about it?'

'Antiseptic. One of the great modern inventions. And some gauze, I expect. Don't look so worried, you won't die of it.'

'Oh, good,' he said, poking experimentally at the wound himself. 'It would be embarrassing to die at this point. That wasn't even the last dragon.'

The Patrician

'This is what comes of leaving the big ones until last,' she chided him.

He came back to her hotel room, and she patched him up, because obviously a two thousand year old man couldn't be trusted with gauze and antiseptic, let alone with the task of going to a doctor.

He had many scars across his torso, though they seemed far older than his skin.

Julius looked longingly at her bed, and Clea rolled her eyes at him. 'Fine, you can stay. When did you last sleep?'

'January,' he said, and was practically snoring before he hit the pillow.

He slept for three days. Clea was afraid he was dying, or hibernating, and she had to change her travel plans to stay in Paris a little longer. Somehow, just leaving him here seemed wrong, especially when there might be vengeful griffins or sphinxes flying in through the window at any moment.

'Thank you,' Julius said on the morning of the third day, and was startled when she leaped up from her armchair, letting books spill across the floor as she came over to kiss him. 'What was that for?'

'I thought you had left me here alone with dragons still on the loose,' she told him.

'Oh,' he said. 'I wouldn't do that. I've been looking forward to crossing off dragons.' And then he kissed her back.

Apparently, she was no longer too young for him, or familiarity had pushed his resistance aside, or something like that. He removed her clothes with a careful precision that made her shiver, and made love to her with an intensity that had her closing her eyes, so that she did not burst into flame.

'If I had known you could do that,' she said, some time later, 'I would have jumped you when I was twenty-five.'

'I like you now,' he said, hands exploring the creases and puckered parts of her stomach, like she was a map he was trying to understand. 'Far more interesting. Children don't appeal to me.'

'I was hardly a child when I was twenty-five,' she said, but of course she had been. She was a child to him now, this tight-bodied, young-looking man who had just brought her to orgasm more times than she could count.

Fifty-three, and she was just starting out. Had only now seen her first dragon. 'How long do you have?' she asked. 'Before you have to go kill things again.'

'Nothing but time,' said Julius, nibbling experimentally on her hipbone. That translated, as it turned out, to three weeks in the hotel, before he disappeared again, on his quest to cross more creatures off that bloody list of his.

Life continued.

V

When she was seventy-two, Clea took her grandchildren to visit the quiet streets of Nova Ostia. Bus tours still took people out there, though there were no more shops and no open thermopolium serving honey cakes and egg salad, no community of families enacting the ancient ways.

'What did you do for internet?' Mercy asked, more interested in the whole thing than her cousins were.

The Patrician

'Oh we had wifi back then,' Clea assured her. 'And plenty of mod cons in most of the homes—where the tourists couldn't see. But we dressed and behaved as authentically as we could, when in public.'

'Weird,' muttered Sebastian, obviously bored.

'Why didn't they just digitise it, Nan?' asked Blake, who wandered through artificial landscapes all the time, thanks to his favourite gaming module.

'They did, eventually,' said Clea. 'It was just ... a lovely thing that existed, once. It all made some sort of sense at the time. It wasn't an ordinary childhood, but it was a good one.'

Clea thought about lamia bites on her brother's neck, of smashing gargoyles on the roofs of the city. She hadn't seen Julius in years. That list of his was getting shorter, on the rare occasions he let her peek at it. Perhaps he had killed the last manticore or basilisk already, and found his peaceful reward.

Perhaps.

Except, no. He hadn't killed the last manticore. Clea stopped and blinked at the creature that prowled the Forum, a bright splash of tawny hide and scarlet claws against the monotone buildings. Head of a lion. Face of ... a person, though it was twisted into something quite ugly. A long, lashing, sting-laden tail.

She began to laugh. 'It really is a manticore. Goodness me. And he said it was a metaphor.'

'Is that one of your tourist things?' Seb asked in alarm. Even Blake turned off his gaming module, staring at the monster.

'It's pretty,' said Mercy.

Clea shushed them. 'Don't move. Everything's going to be fine.'

It was too long since she had fought monsters. She didn't know the first thing about weapons that would work against a manticore, and here she was armed with nothing but her handbag and three grandchildren.

She should have thought of this. Should have remembered that coming home wasn't just nostalgia and honey cakes. Nova Ostia drew the monsters to it with these old borrowed stones.

The manticore strutted closer, poised to pounce. Its human face growled.

An arrow thunked deeply into its side, and then another. A third took it through the side of its head, dropping it to the ground.

'This place comes with superheroes!' yelled Mercy, and the boys cheered.

Clea looked up, shading her face from the sun, and saw a familiar silhouette in a broad-brimmed hat, standing on the roof of the temple of Saturn. She waved, and he waved back.

'Who's that, Nan?' asked Mercy.

'A very dear friend,' she said, and walked neatly around the manticore. 'Come on. I'll show you where I used to live.'

It was the last time, and she didn't realise it, though every time she had seen him in the last decade she had thought, 'This could be the last time.' She wasn't going to live forever, after all. Seventy-two full and healthy years, two children, three grandchildren, it had been a good life, and barely an interlude in his.

The Patrician

'Just don't train my granddaughter up as a monster hunter,' she had said to him in Paris a year ago, though she knew secretly that Mercy would probably be rather good at the task once she got over the shock.

'Who do you think I am, Peter Pan?' said Julius, as if the very idea was distasteful to him. They finished sipping their wine, and went upstairs together, and said no more of it.

That had been the last time they would speak, but she didn't know that, either.

Clea got the call four days before her seventy-fifth birthday. 'Sydney?' said Poppy in protest, when she heard about it. 'Mum, you can't. Not all the way to Australia again!'

But who else was going to go?

At the end of a long flight, Clea met with some sympathetic police officers and morgue attendants. They apologised for bringing her all this way, and she apologised for putting them to any trouble, and what with one thing and another, they filled the corridors with empty noise.

She had hoped it wouldn't be him. You always do in moments like that, don't you? A mistake, plain and simple. But she had flown a long way in the hope of proving the police officers wrong.

He had carried no identification, just his notebook, and her name. They showed it to her when they passed over his other belongings (a few papers, a safe deposit key, a greened-bronze necklace) and there were contact details too, all the addresses she had lived at over the years, the phone numbers, each one crossed out as a new one was added.

Love and Romanpunk   *Tansy Rayner Roberts*

Julius had never visited her at any of her homes, never written, never called. The world had thrown them together countless times, and they were happy with that. But he could have found her any time he wanted to.

There was no one else in the notebook. Perhaps there had been, in other centuries, in other notebooks or wax tablets or whatever he used before the book, but in this one there was only Clea Majora, later Clea Robinson, and the list of crossed-off items. Basilisk, Chimaera, Dragon…

One item was not crossed out—Gorgon. It must have been the last creature that he killed. Did his family curse not even allow him a moment to catch his breath and tidy his notebook before he fell?

Clea looked down at his calm, still body. Gorgons killed by turning you to stone, didn't they? That wasn't what had ended him. His skin was waxy and grey, but undeniably human.

He seemed young. Twenty-nine, he had been when his aging stopped, if his dates were correct. So young. She did not remember when they had appeared the same age. Julius had never been one to worry unduly about the physical realities of time. He had shown little romantic interest in her until she looked far older than he. Then again, he was two thousand years old. Even now, she was young, in comparison.

'Was he a friend of your son?' asked a police officer, who obviously meant to be kind.

Clea swallowed any number of retorts. What could she say that would sum up this man? 'He was a friend,' she said, finally.

***

The Patrician

VI

She had his ashes buried in Nova Ostia. It should have been Rome, really, but where was there space for a headstone in Rome? Here at least, in an abandoned city made with authentic stone, she could have some control over how his deeds were recorded. It was a large slab of paving stone that matched the whiteness of the buildings, and she laid it at the foot of the Temple of Augustus.

JULIUS, OF THE JULIAS
SON OF GAIUS CAESAR CALIGULA
HUNTER OF BEASTS
SLAYER OF MONSTERS
FRIEND OF CLEA MAJORA

It was not enough. Not nearly enough. But what more could she do? She could surround it with carvings of lamia and werewolves and manticores, but it would mean nothing to anyone who followed.

She buried him with his sword, the *gladius* that had aged as little as he had. There were other belongings which she could have placed in his grave—the necklace, or his list of monsters, or the painstakingly copied-out manuscript she had found, all in Latin, which she rather thought had been authored by one of his aunts. Julius had collected all manner of ephemera in his lifetime—a claw, a vial of silver blood, a sheath of dragon skin. Trophies which meant nothing, now.

When Clea was gone, there would be no one who remembered who he had been, what he had done, and for just one moment, that thought was utterly unbearable.

Then she breathed, and looked around. She was an old woman standing in an ancient city, barely a step away from the Australian bush. The world was full of wonders, and possibilities.

'Find peace,' she said aloud, and walked away.

There would be more adventures in the years to come.

Last of the Romanpunks

'It's been a long time, Sebastian,' said Eloise, making what I used to call her 'kitten' face, back when I liked her.

'Yeah, that was deliberate on my part,' I replied.

Her brother Brian, who was responsible for this unexpected reunion of ours, looked embarrassed. So he should.

Eloise stood in front of me, glistening in a beaded stola, sandaled feet flip-flopping on the mosaic tiles, her blonde hair pinned up in so many curls it made my own scalp hurt. She had a sunny, 'the world is my oyster' sort of smile, and she looked like the sweetest person in the universe.

Appearances can be deceptive.

The waitress arrived with a jug of spiced wine, red like blood, which she poured into cups decorated with plastic gladiators impaled on toothpicks. I knew how the poor buggers felt.

'Thank you, dear,' said Eloise. 'What a charming thing you've done to your uniform. Don't let me see you do it again.'

Every waitress in this bar was dressed like a Roman slave girl, all tiny white tunics and blonde hair in ringlets as they moved from the bar to the couches with effortless ease, bringing cups of wine to the customers. This one was brunette, sulky, and had pulled on a pair of jeans under her tunic.

'Yes, boss,' she said, with restrained venom.

So this crazy floating taverna was Eloise's. I should have known when I first heard that some nutter had bought an airship to launch an Ancient-Roman-themed bar, let alone when I first set foot on board and one of the pretty blonde waitresses tried to wrap me in a toga. Romanpunk had always been Ellie's thing. She and her friends were so far into the subculture that I could hardly see them for grape stems and scrolls of elegiac poetry. Believe me, there's only so many times a bloke can take being compared to Julius Caesar.

Of all the watered wine joints in all the world, I had to let myself be trapped on this one. The newly christened Julia Augusta was a two hour round trip across the Sydney skies. It was entirely automated—no human pilot or engineers at the helm, and it's bloody impossible to bribe a computer to let you off early.

I was well and truly stuck. One hour, forty-five minutes to go.

'There's a triple tip in it for you if you get me a cup of arsenic right now,' I muttered to the surly brunette waitress.

'An asp in a covered basket is more period-appropriate,' she shot back. 'I'll see what I can do.' Such a tease.

Eloise lowered herself to the couch opposite, making sure to flash a discreet amount of her admittedly awesome cleavage. 'Sorry about the little deception, sweetie. Would you have come if I had called?'

'I'm still considering my chances if I leap off this zeppelin mid-flight,' I replied, not bothering to be polite. I'd let Brian, who I thought was a mate, lure me here on the promise of

Last of the Romanpunks

a job. Instead, I had to endure my ex-girlfriend's jabs for an hour and forty-three minutes.

Eloise's lower lip wobbled a little. 'I was sorry to hear about your nan.'

'Well, that fixes everything.'

'I liked her,' Brian put in. Eloise looked at him as if he had said something stupid. 'What? She was a great old lady. Always nice to me.'

I'd spent the whole day dealing with the aftermath of some nonk breaking into my dead grandmother's house and stealing several of the weirder pieces of my inheritance. The last thing I wanted was to discuss her with these two. 'She was ninety. It happens.'

Brian took a deep, nervous gulp from his wine cup, and pushed one towards me. 'Do you want water with yours, Seb? Spices?'

'Romans were fucking barbarians,' I replied.

'A simple "no" would have sufficed.'

The waitress came back and put a clay cup in front of me. It contained several inches of very un-Roman neat whiskey. 'Best I could do on short notice. We're all out of snakes.'

I took a slow sip and did my best not to stare at her legs (the lack of jeans was a definite improvement) as she stomped away. 'Starting to hate this bar a little less.'

Eloise was still smiling. Made me wonder if there was arsenic in my cup after all. 'We really do have a job offer for you.'

'Not interested.'

'Are things going so well in the insurance investigation business?'

Things sucked severely. The world prefers to catch their fraudsters on street cameras and Google Earth these days. No one appreciates an artist like they used to. If my bank account dropped any lower, I was going to have to go back to spying on cheating husbands. Some professions never die out, and as luck would have it they tend to be the really depressing ones.

'I do all right,' I lied.

One hour, thirty-eight minutes.

Eloise toyed with her gladiator toothpick, and added water and spices to her wine. When she was sure I was watching her, she drank with great deliberation, staining her lips. 'Are you going to listen to my proposal?'

'Nope.' I stood up, nursing my whiskey cup. The smell of cinnamon and wine was making my stomach curdle. 'This little reunion has been fun, but I think I'm going to go queue for the exit.'

Eloise looked up at me, and it wasn't her kitten face any more. 'I can make you stay, Seb. With one word.'

'No offence, sweetheart, but it's going to have to be one hell of a word.' I glanced at Brian, who looked away in embarrassment. Yeah, he and I were going to have words of our own, one of these days. If I ever spoke to him again. Family is family, I get that, but mates don't trick other mates into getting stranded on their ex-girlfriend's airship.

Eloise smiled, shaking back her golden curls. Don't ask me how she still had a slinky figure under that white sack of a Roman matron's garment—but push up bras are definitely out of period. She wetted her lips, to prolong the moment. 'Lamia,' she said.

The ship tilted.

I was back in my seat, gripping my cup with whiskey-splashed fingertips. 'That's not even funny.'

She was no longer pretending to flirt with me. This was the real Eloise, the stone cold bitch I had run, not walked, away from. 'We're going to change the world, Seb. And you're going to help us.'

La·mi·a

n. pl. la·mi·as or la·mi·ae

1. *Greek Mythology*. A monster represented as a serpent with the head and breasts of a woman that ate children and sucked the blood from men.

2. A female vampire, daemon or sorceress.

3. The eponymous heroine of *Lamia*, an unpublished novel by Mary Wollstonecraft Godwin (1797-1815). Lady Lamia Worthington had silver blood and could take the shape of a woman or a snake. She fed on the blood of a series of young husbands, and gave birth to a monstrous daughter who literally consumed her.

4. A really completely not-fucking-mythological creature which survived until the twenty-first century, when the last two in existence attempted to feed upon a teenage boy and were wiped from the face of the earth by my nan, Clea Majora Jackson, and a man she only ever referred to in her stories as 'Julius'. In my family, we call him the monster-killer.

'Right,' I said finally, licking whiskey from my fingers, because I didn't want to waste a drop. 'You have my attention. Let's start with an easy one, shall we? The items that were stolen from my nan's house this week. Any chance you know anything about that?'

'That depends on your definition of theft,' said my darling ex. 'Your nan had been illegally hoarding some important historical artefacts, Sebastian. All those weapons. Jewellery—quite valuable ancient pieces, many of them. But the worst crime of all ... scholars have known of the existence of Agrippina's family history for centuries, but it was presumed destroyed. You can't keep a book like that in a box under the bed. It should be in a museum.'

'So that's what you've done, of course,' I said flatly. 'Handed it all into a museum, for the sake of posterity.'

'Oh, I will,' Eloise promised, eyes wide. 'Eventually.' She shifted, and I saw the glint of a dull greened-with-age necklace that I had last seen in my nan's safe. It was a depiction of three Julias—Agrippina, Drusilla and Livilla, sisters of Caligula. It was precious to my family. It belonged to my cousin Mercy now, not this bitch I had once loved.

Fuck, fuck, fuck. Never mind the necklace. Most of what she had taken had no value but family nostalgia. But the book was dynamite. Mercy and Blake were going to kill me. 'Some things are too bloody dangerous to allow out in public, Ellie.'

'Didn't do a very good job of guarding it, then, did you?' she said prettily.

Brian was staring at the floor, wallowing in his own embarrassment.

This wasn't just my ex out for some kind of twisted revenge against my family. This was serious. 'What exactly do you plan to do?' I asked.

Eloise had never looked so beautiful. 'I plan to become immortal, darling. And I want you to stand at my side.'

I laughed. 'Immortality? You know who doesn't want immortality? Immortals. My nan hung out with a two thousand year old bloke for most of her life, and the message she got from it? Not the lifestyle choice of the future. Getting old is what we do. It's what makes us human.'

'Tell him, Brian,' Eloise said, back to being the ice queen.

He looked at me, and now that I was paying attention, I could see how tired he was. 'Terese is sick,' he said, and I heard despair in every word.

Fuck. 'I'm sorry to hear that,' I said, trying not to get distracted by the thought of bubbly Terese and her two awesome children. 'I understand. You want to do everything you can. But this isn't on the list. It's not an acceptable option, for anyone. A good man fought for forty times his natural lifespan, to rid the world of monsters. There's no reason big or important enough to bring them back.'

'You'd do it if it was Mercy,' said Eloise. 'You'd do it in a second.'

I thought of my brilliant, brave cousin. She made detective before she was twenty-six. She's devoted her life to being a fucking hero, and she's the last member of our family who believes in justice, and love, and all that crap. She's the best person I know. 'If Mercy tried to turn herself into a lamia,' I said in a calm, patient voice, 'I'd put a bullet in her head. If she was dying and I was the one trying to turn her into a monster? She'd be the one handy with the bullet.'

'I'm really sorry,' said Eloise, with a sigh. 'It's far too late for bullets. But there is still time for you to change your mind.

I hope you do. You're a little too old to be food.'

I could hear my heartbeat hammering against my chest. I felt the change in the room, like a sigh, or a hiss. Over there, by the bar, I could see the surly waitress arguing with customers. They leaned in towards her, three of them, beautiful women with flat, distant faces. In this light, their eyes seemed silver.

How had I not noticed before now that every customer in the bar was blonde, and female?

I stared back at the wine carafe, and then back to two people I had once thought of as family. 'It's in the wine, isn't it?'

Lamia blood. Of all the stupid talismans for my Nan to keep. But she kept every fragment that had belonged to Julius the monster-killer. How do you dispose of lamia blood safely? Here's a tip: don't spike a whole bar's worth of wine with those devious silver droplets. Unless you want a zeppelin full of silver-blooded vampiric women soaring over your city.

Apparently that was exactly what my Ellie wanted.

The waitress screamed. As I turned in her direction, she swung a long-necked brandy bottle around in an arc, smashing it over the head of a Roman matrona who was wrapped around her like a predatory squid, arms everywhere. The other waitresses, the blonde ones, gathered around, not helping her. Their eyes were silver too.

I guess she'd been sulking too much to drink the wine.

'Don't fight it,' said Eloise, moving to my side. She had a cup of that damned grape juice in her hand, holding it out to me like there was a chance in hell I was going to take it from

Last of the Romanpunks

her. 'We're changing the world, Seb. You can be a part of it.'

'With you as the queen of everything, I suppose,' I said flatly.

She laughed, a low familiar sound, and I could hear the change in her already. 'Of course.'

'Sorry, love, but I walked away from that world already.'

The waitress was fighting them off as best she could, with a broken bottle in each hand now, but they closed in on her. A dozen or more circled the bar, and others were awakening, one by one, on every couch in the room.

She was the only one who counted as food. Her, and me, and I still had Eloise hanging onto my arm, marking me out as company property. If I gave up Ellie's idea of protection, I'd have a horde of glamorous vixens on my neck in under a minute, and while that kind of death might look good on paper it lacked appeal right now.

A hand brushed against my other arm, and I jumped. It was Brian, looking wan and silvery. Not sure if the lamia blood was agreeing with him like it was with Eloise, but I didn't have a lot of sympathy for the bloke right now. 'Terese going to be proud of you for setting off this epidemic, is she?' I snapped.

'I didn't have a choice.'

'Stupidest sentence I've ever heard.' My mind was racing ahead of my mouth. It was here, all of it. Contained on a floating vessel. I'd read everything my nan had kept on the bad old days of monsters under the bed, including her own notes on what she had witnessed in her lifetime. How do you kill lamia?

Fire, baby. Flame and swords.

Was I up for that? I uncovered insurance fraud for a living. Was I capable of setting a whole fucking zeppelin alight, dooming my ex-girlfriend and her brother, as well as the only other person in the bar who was still what I would call human? Was I strong enough to take us all down in flames?

As I hesitated, the waitress punched one of the swarming blondes in the face, stabbed another in the arm with her broken bottle, then ran and locked herself in what was either a storage room or a large cupboard. I hoped for her sake there was a window and a really long rope ladder back there.

'Hold him,' said Eloise, and Brian's hands clamped around my wrists, pinning both arms behind my back. He was cool to the touch. I was struggling to remember Nan's stories, which had always seemed so removed from relevance, plus all the vampire movies I'd ever seen. Keeping the details separate would probably save my life. Garlic, for instance, could be added to the list of things that were no help whatsoever.

It was a hell of a long list.

Eloise strode grandly to the centre of the room. She shook her hair back, enjoying the attention as the faux-Romans turned to her, hissing their approval. 'You all know me. You all made your choice. We are the future of this world.'

'Food,' whispered one, and they all took up the call. 'Food. Foooood.' A whole lot of silver eyes were fixed on me.

'He will remain intact for now,' said my ex, making sure to stress the 'for now' in case I was in any doubt about my impending doom. 'I know you are hungry, my darlings, but think of it. In twenty minutes, we will be settling down at the Opera House Platform. So much real food, young food. Bored and available.'

The Opera House Platform was on the roof of the largest shopping centre in the country. It was school holidays. *Harry Potter and the Lost Generation* was playing on an endless loop until midnight and lamia, I remembered now, had a particular taste for teenagers. Wonderful.

We had to crash and burn before that. Hell, crashing into the Platform and all the deaths that might cause was small potatoes compared to what would happen if the lamia were loosed on the world again. Julius was dead. There were no more legendary Roman heroes waiting to save the day for the rest of us mortals. There was just me.

Eloise gestured wildly, enjoying the attention of her minions. 'In honour of this momentous day, I shall take a new name worthy of your leader. From now on, I shall be known as Julia Agrippina Augusta Lamia!'

This time, they hissed their approval so loudly, it sounded like a freak hailstorm.

Bullshit, said a voice inside my head. It took me a few seconds to realise that it wasn't just my own internal thoughts.

Who the fuck are you?

You wouldn't believe me if I told you. The voice was older, female, and smug, and oddly familiar.

...Nan?

Don't be ridiculous, she said haughtily, from somewhere between my cerebral cortex and my migraine. *I am the original Julia Agrippina, daughter of Germanicus.*

Now it was my turn to think: *Bullshit!*

I assure you, young man...

Why aren't you speaking Latin?

Because I'm using your brain. It requires use of your own limited vocabulary. She sounded impatient. *This will never work if you don't believe me. Pay attention.*

My head was suddenly full of her. I was overwhelmed by a musty montage of Ancient Rome, the smells and tastes. In the space of a few seconds I tasted honey for the first time, swam through salt water to kill a man I hated, screamed as a baby squeezed its way out of me, and stuck a bronze *gladius* through the body of a dragon.

When those seconds were over I was left sweating and gasping for breath, still held tight by Brian, and believing every word that the witch inside my head had spoken.

Why me? I stared across the room at the artist formerly known as Eloise. *She's the one wearing your necklace.*

Have you seen the inside of that woman's brain?

Intimately.

I'd rather die. Besides, you will be far more useful.

If you're the Agrippina who wrote that book my nan looked after all those years—you're just as much lamia as my ex-girlfriend. The whole imperial family was polluted with silver blood. I'm not stupid.

That silver blood was the shame of my family, she said crisply, sounding more like a stern teacher I had in Grade Five than the ghost of a long-dead Empress. *My sisters and I trained young Julius and cursed him to be our hands once we were gone from the earth, to be the redemption of the Caesars. He has gone to his peace too soon, and that leaves you and I to sweep up the crumbs.*

Last of the Romanpunks

***

I only saw Julius the monster-killer once, when I was eight or so. He slayed a manticore in front of my brother Blake, my cousin Mercy and me. I'd never seen anything cooler in my life. After that, I begged Nan for the stories, and she let them out one at a time, reluctantly, like they were pieces of something she had no right to share.

When I was an adult, she told the stories differently. She told me of his sacrifice, the man who lived two thousand years, picking off the monsters of the world one by one. The last of the Caesars, bastard son of a fucking evil family.

Towards the end, when her memory couldn't be trusted, when the nurses didn't even like her to make a cup of tea on her own because she would forget the teabag or scald herself with the hot water, Nan told me the stories a third time, and the details were note-perfect even as everything else went fuzzy around her. She couldn't remember whether I was Seb or Blake, but she knew the five pressure points to go for if you needed to slay a griffin.

I listened to her then because it calmed her down to think that someone was going to remember Julius and the family he had come from. 'I'm glad your mothers didn't call you Julia,' she said once to Mercy. 'There's a power in that name. The Julias were warriors, soldiers, and heroes. Mad, cursed and doomed, every one of them.'

Now I had one of them in my head. Julia Agrippina, Bitch of Rome. Murderer of Emperors. Part lamia, part werewolf, part nagging old cow.

She wasn't just in my head. She was in my fucking veins. I was glad Brian was still holding my hands behind me, because it was like I couldn't even remember how to walk in this big, clumsy male body.

This had better be temporary or I was going to have to punch someone.

We have much to do, Agrippina said inside my head. *Where is my nephew's gladius?* She punctuated the word with a visual image of a battered bronze short sword, like I was too stupid to know what the word meant.

Buried with him, I told her. Nan was thorough. If there was half a chance there were still any monsters in the world, she wanted to make sure us kids were never going to be tempted to hunt them down.

Agrippina made liberal use of my excellent swearing vocabulary.

'Brian,' I said in a quiet voice. 'You know these wenches are going to eat me, right? That's what lamia do.' Mostly they eat children, but I'm pretty sure my blood would do in a pinch.

'They're not the only ones,' Brian said in a ragged voice. 'I'm part of it now too, Seb.'

I twisted around to look at him. Yeah. He was all pasty, and there was a glittery sheen to his skin. 'It's not too late,' I said to him.

Of course it's too late, Agrippina chided. *He drank the blood of a lamia. What did he think it was going to do to him?*

'No,' I said aloud. 'Those papers Eloise stole? I know them by heart. Lamia biology changed in the Victorian era, with the Wollstonecraft baby. You weren't born to this,

Last of the Romanpunks

Brian. If you don't feed in a day or so, the lamia blood will just burn away. All you have to do is hang in there, and not bite anyone.'

He looked at me apologetically, and I made the mistake of meeting his gaze. His silver eyes burned into me and I couldn't move. Fuck. Lamia skills. 'I'm sorry,' said Brian. 'But I have to do this properly. I have to take it back to her.'

I couldn't prevent him from leaning in, almost nuzzling his face against my collarbone, and then he bit hard, and it hurt, it fucking hurt, and that was enough to break me out of whatever hypnotic shit he had worked on me. I cracked him over the top of the head with my fist and he fell back, his mouth wet with my blood.

His reflexes weren't great. Maybe it was the whiskey in my blood—though it couldn't be doing much for me either. I ran towards the bar, vaulting over it as the horde of beautiful blondes hissed and slithered towards me.

'Stop it!' cried Eloise, halting them for a moment. Aww, she did love me. 'His blood isn't pure enough. If we are to bring the lamia back to full strength, you must feed upon children, all of you.' So much for old times' sake.

The lamia women hesitated, staring at the ragged wound on my neck, which still hurt, damn it. Brian didn't have the juice yet to do the traditional lamia thing and make the feeding taste feel good. Or maybe he was just a second rate monster and always would be.

Trying not to look into any of their eyes, I hammered on the storeroom door, hoping for my own sake the brunette waitress was still there and not hanging out the back window on a rope ladder made from her own Levis.

Forty-five minutes left. We had forty-five minutes before this boat landed and the massacre began.

'Let me the hell in!' I yelled into the storeroom.

'Do you think I'm stupid?' the surly waitress yelled back.

Huh. She had a point.

Fire will kill them, Agrippina said inside my mind as the lamia women hovered between obeying their leader and following the delicious scent of my bleeding neck.

Way ahead of you on that one. If only I had two sticks to rub together. I let my head fall back against the dense wood of the door. 'Typical. I had to fall for a girl who liked romanpunk. I couldn't have gotten entangled with a cultist, or a part time assassin, or a meth addict. No, I had to go for the pretty girl in sandals who had a thing about Virgil and roast dormice and becoming *the queen of the immortal snake women.*'

The door snapped open, and I fell backwards into the storeroom. The waitress immediately shut the door behind me, wedging a long shelf along it for extra security.

'How did you know I wasn't one of them?' I said, looking up at her.

She made a face and pushed her dark hair behind her ears. 'You're just so pathetic.'

Excellent. I sat up. 'What do we have for weapons?'

'Three vacuum packs of marinated olives.'

'We're going to die, then.'

'Looks like.'

Only, we weren't going to die. The lamia weren't that interested in us. We could probably hide out here in safety until the automated airship touched down on the Opera

House Platform, and the lamia invasion of Earth began.

'What's your name?' I asked her.

The waitress sighed and sat next to me on the floor. 'Jools.'

Caught by surprise, I started to laugh. 'For real?'

She scowled at me. 'What's so funny?'

'You're a Julia.'

'I guess.' She looked like she was seriously beginning to regret letting the blood-stained madman in to share the prison with her. 'It's just a name.'

Sure, it was just a name. Women's first names were chosen randomly these days. They weren't a marker of what family you belonged to. The chances of this surly waitress being descended from the Julii Caesars was minimal, to say the least. But it meant something. It had to mean something that she was here.

'We've got to fight back,' I told her. I owed it to Julius, to Nan, and to the decrepit old dead woman in my head.

I'm not going to say Jools looked at me like I was crazy, but that's only because she hadn't looked at me any other way for a while now. It was our thing. 'How do you suggest we do that?'

Blood. Lamia blood was the key. It had to be. If we could stop the airship from touching down for long enough, the lamia wouldn't be able to feed, and they'd go back to being human. Or they'd faint from starvation.

As long as we didn't let any more of them gnaw on our necks.

'Ever fancied hijacking an airship?' I asked Jools.

That's my boy, said Agrippina in my head.

Love and Romanpunk   *Tansy Rayner Roberts*

✳✳✳

It looks kind of easy in vids when the hero squeezes through air vents or whatever, without rumpling his combat suit. Whoever designed airships did not give sufficient consideration to future insurance investigators and waitresses who might be trying to save the world.

I wriggled myself along a narrow space at about three inches per minute. My bruises had bruises on them, and Jools was muttering the whole time about how oh no, she couldn't just take a job on a sushi train like a normal person, she had to pick the flying Romanpunk bar that was trying to kill her…

My phone chimed and it took some serious gymnastics to slide it out of my pocket. 'Merce? Not a great time.'

'Seb, don't hang up, have you seen Eloise lately?'

I barked a short laugh. 'You might say that. Has your department got any pull with the Army? Or the Air Force?'

As usual, Mercy barrelled through without actually listening to me. 'The sergeant investigating the robbery at Nan's house is trying to connect it to another recent crime—they have CCTV footage of your Eloise breaking into a grave, out bush.'

That stopped me. I lay perfectly still in the air vent, breathing hard. 'Nova Ostia.' The old Roman replica city in the middle of nowhere. Nan grew up there, and that was where she had buried Julius the monster-killer.

'Yes.' Mercy sounded tinny and far away.

'She took the fucking sword.' I hadn't seen it in the bar. Where was Eloise hiding it?

'There's a sword?' Jools said from a metre or so behind me.

Last of the Romanpunks

I want that gladius *back*, Agrippina hissed inside my head.

'Merce, get onto Blake,' I said urgently.

'Your brother's useless with this stuff...' she complained.

'Yeah, but he has a double degree in engineering and computer hacking, and I'm going to need him to find the specs for the Julia Augusta airship. She's about to dock in the next twenty minutes or so, and we need to stop that happening, or Eloise is going to lead a gang of newly-blooded lamia out to eat all the prettiest teenagers they can find.'

There was a long pause on the other end of the phone.

'Seriously?' Mercy said finally.

I wanted to scream at her. 'No, this is an overly elaborate prank. Don't I sound serious? I need Blake to work out how I can override this fucker and steer it out to sea, and I need *you* to use your police credentials to evacuate the Opera House Platform and help me save the world. If it's not too much trouble.'

'I'll give him a call then,' she said, sounding shocked.

'You do that.' I clicked the phone shut and started wriggling again. 'Almost there.'

'You have a cop *and* a computer hacker in the family?' Jools asked.

'Nan liked to plan ahead.'

I pushed open the hatch and half fell, half jumped down into the small, triangular control room. I was expecting banks of flashing lights and switches and dials, but I guess I'd been watching the wrong kind of vids. Everything was smooth and empty, apart from a couple of touch screens and the view of the city beneath us. I could see the Opera House Platform, only a few minutes away.

Something slammed into me from behind, knocking me against the wall. My phone skittered across the floor, out of reach. Brian. Fucker. He was stronger than before, and hissing between his teeth like a reptile. I looked up to see Eloise dragging Jools down out of the hatch. She held the bronze *gladius* in one hand, pressing the edge against Jools' neck.

It was a short, unimpressive weapon. No rust or green corrosion on it, and it was in pretty good condition considering it had been slaying monsters for two thousand years. I'd seen similar swords in museums, crumbling pieces that would never take another edge. But this one was different. This *gladius* had been bathed in the blood of dozens of different monsters. It was the sword of Julius.

If Jools survived this, I was going to recommend a tetanus shot.

Agrippina hissed like a lamia inside my skull.

'You don't want to do that,' I said aloud. 'Her blood isn't pure enough, right?'

'I wanted to do this properly,' Eloise said in a pouty voice. 'This is all your fault, Seb. If you could have just let me wait to feed on the perfect victim, I could be the most powerful lamia who has ever lived. But I'll settle for living forever.' She leaned down, her teeth sharp as she came close to the blade.

Jools let out a tiny gasp, and the edge of the *gladius* sank deeper.

My phone, on the other side of the room, chimed and then beeped at incoming data. I couldn't reach it.

'We're almost there,' I said. 'Wait for your perfect victim—it's only a few minutes.'

'This is your fault,' Eloise said, and bit down. She was better at it than Brian had been. Jools cried out only once and then her eyes glazed over, like it felt good. Her body fell limply against Eloise, who was drinking deep.

Eloise only needed a mouthful to bring her full powers on, to make herself a lamia forever. But I had no faith she was planning to stop there.

My fucking sword, Agrippina snarled in my head.

So take it, I demanded, furious at her for letting this get so far.

The control room blurred before my eyes as the Bitch of Rome took control of my body. I fought it for a moment and then tried to relax into it. I wasn't doing too well at this hero thing. Let one of the original Julias take the wheel.

If you know anything about Julia Agrippina, you probably know that she was part of the imperial family of Rome. She's famous for being one of Caligula's feistier sisters, exiled more than once because she spoke her mind in his presence. Then she married her own uncle Claudius, the next emperor, and poisoned him with a dish of mushrooms. You might even have heard about how her own son, the Emperor Nero, tried to kill her many times over. Not a popular lass, our Agrippina.

Only, there's more to the story than that. The truth is that Agrippina and her two sisters were like secret agents and paranormal bodyguards to their brother. They fought monsters and assassins. After he was gone, they raised his son in secret, training him for his future.

They turned Julius into the monster-killer he was. I don't know if they cursed him, or just prepared him for what he had to do, but they're the reason he was as good as he was. So I guess they saved the world too, more than once.

Agrippina knocked Brian back against the wall with my elbow, then did something with my leg that I didn't think was even anatomically possible, and when he head-butted me in the chest, she wrapped my hands firmly around his neck, and oh fuck, oh fuck, I felt it through my fingers. I—she—we snapped Brian's neck. My hands shook with the sensation of his bones breaking, but we were still going, my limbs as our weapons.

Eloise threw Jools to one side to fight us, but Agrippina scoffed at the amateurish hold she had on the *gladius*. She dodged with my body, weaved, spun, and I felt my hand wrench the hilt from Eloise.

Her eyes glowed silver and she lunged for me, faster than any human could. But Agrippina was inside me, and she wasn't human either. I was caught between the two of them, unable to do anything, except when Agrippina brought the sword swinging around to behead Eloise. I flinched, using every strength I had to pull the sword back, away, to stop it happening.

Don't fight me, boy, Agrippina demanded, her voice filling me from edge to edge.

I can't kill her.

What did you think we were doing here, teaching her a stern lesson? She's a monster! Let me do this for you.

Eloise backed away slowly, eyes on me. 'Don't do it, Seb. We can be together again. Forever.'

'Yeah, okay, Agrippina,' I said aloud. 'You can behead her now.'

'Don't play the tough guy, no one believes it,' Eloise said, sneering at me. 'All mouth, no guts.' She lashed out a hand, smashing through the plastic window as if it was porcelain. 'I'm blooded. I'm stronger than you can imagine. We're only a few metres above the platform. I can jump from here, and you can't stop me.'

'Wouldn't be too sure of that,' said another voice. I looked up, and saw Jools over by the control panels. She was white as a ghost and had a bloody mark on her neck that matched mine, but she was holding my phone and looking pleased with herself. 'Seb, your brother says "hi".'

Blake had come through with a hack, then. About fucking time.

Eloise let out a screech of rage and leaped up on to the ledge as if she was a cat. The cold air streaming into the control room caught her blonde curls, so they flew up like a halo around her face. The green necklace stood out against her pale skin and fluttering white stola. We were over the harbour, nothing but water below us, and steadily climbing.

Route changed. No platform below us.

'Oh, I'm sorry,' said Jools politely. 'Did we rob you of the chance to snack on random teenagers? Probably for the best. Have you seen all that purple makeup the emos are pasting on this season? I bet they taste terrible.'

I let Agrippina raise the *gladius* with my hand, pointing it at Eloise. 'We stay up here until that silver blood wears off every one of your lamia army.'

Eloise smiled, and shook her head at me. Yeah, she was still cute. I'm only human. 'Not this time, Seb. I have a promise to keep, to Brian's wife.'

I heard him behind me, a low hiss, and half turned around before Brian smacked into me, broken neck cracking back into place. Fuck, lamia. Beheading works, neck-breaking doesn't. Something to remember in future.

Brian and I struggled with the *gladius*. I didn't think I could kill him, not by choice. Not again. Terese was such a sweetheart.

He tried to bite my neck again. This was serious, and my head was getting in the way of staying alive. *One more time*, I begged Agrippina, barely a whisper of a thought. One I'd feel guilty about for the rest of my life.

She took me over again and this time, she took his head.

Then it was done, and I was standing in a pool of Brian's blood, and Agrippina was gone. Maybe she had never been there, maybe she was just some fucking hallucination brought on by whiskey and stress and vampires.

Silver blood. There was nothing red about this sticky substance all over the floor. Two hours ago, he had been human.

'She's gone,' Jools said in a low voice, and I looked up to see nothing but a broken plastic window.

'Reckon she survived the drop?' I asked, trying not to sound like I was about to cry or faint or something unmanly like that.

Last of the Romanpunks

'If I've learned one thing about lamia today, it's that they always come back,' she said.

Yeah. That. So much for saving the world.

The police used gas to get us out. Knocked out the lamia-in-waiting, and us too. We woke up in hospital beds with a whole stack of paperwork to fill out. Mercy was teetering somewhere between getting herself fired from the police force, and getting some kind of promotion.

She refused to lie to the press about what was going on. The police had decided to set up some kind of special task force to go after Eloise, and Mercy was big on telling the world all about it. 'Two thousand years of silence didn't get us a monster-free world,' she insisted. The best way to honour Julius now, and to continue his work, is to tell his story.' I wasn't sure I agreed with that, but Mercy had confiscated all of Nan's papers including Agrippina's book. I sensed a publishing deal in her future, if Blake didn't get the jump on her by blogging about it.

They had taken their inheritance, and I was left with the *gladius*.

The bronze short sword had been cleaned, and was lying on my bedside table in the hospital room. No one, not nurses, not police, not even Mercy seemed to notice it. So, it was mine, then.

On the day they released us from hospital and police custody, Jools and I stood together outside the big white doors, blinking our eyes in the sunshine.

'So what was that thing with my name?' she asked, cutting through the awkwardness like it was only in my head. 'When

I first told you what it was, you laughed at me.'

'Oh. Our family kind of has a tradition that women with the name Julia are—kind of superheroes. Warriors, soldiers, hunters … basically they're mighty.'

It sounded stupid when you said it out loud, though Jools didn't seem to think so. She looked thoughtful, and then she smiled for the first time since I'd met her. 'I like that. *Mighty*. I tell you what, next time your crazy ex tries to take over the world or raises an army of the undead or whatever, why don't you give me a call?'

She walked away, still smiling. I watched her go.

I still want my necklace back, Agrippina said, inside my head.

You again.

We have unfinished business, you and I.

If that unfinished business involves monsters and swordfighting, I'm busy that day. But I couldn't take my eyes off Jools disappearing around a corner up ahead, returning to whatever life she had before she took the job on the Romanpunk airship.

Give me a call, she'd said. But, you know, only if there were lamia to fight.

I suppose there were worse fates than hunting monsters. It was a family tradition, after all. With a Julia by my side and another in my head, how could I go wrong?

I took a deep breath, and started walking. *Okay, Agrippina. Where do we start?*

Afterword

There is no Nova Ostia in Australia.

The poet had many sisters, but not that one.

(And besides, it was a different poet.)

Fanny Wollstonecraft was collateral damage but not actually food.

Julia is just a name.

Fiction is always composed of lies, but some are greater and more impertinent lies than others.

Some authors believe that putting words or deeds into the mouths of people who really lived is beyond the pale. I suspect that I am one of those authors, which makes what I have done with this book rather ... uncomfortable. It was, however, an utterly delicious discomfort.

I believe that if everyone who ever wrote an academic thesis followed it up with a tasty piece of fiction that is the literary equivalent of spraying offensive graffiti tags all over their area of expertise, the world would be a better place.

Agrippina did write a secret history of her family, one of many essential documents which was easily lost and never found again. I suspect it did not feature lamia, manticores or werewolves. Then again, you never know.

I regret nothing.

About the Author

Tansy Rayner Roberts lives in Tasmania with her partner and two daughters. She has a PhD in Classics, and specialised in the study of Roman imperial women. Tansy blogs at <u>tansyrr.com</u> and is one of the voices of the feminist SF podcast Galactic Suburbia.

Tansy's Creature Court trilogy: *Power and Majesty* (2010), *The Shattered City* (2011) and *Reign of Beasts* (to be released in late 2011) is available from HarperCollins Voyager. Tansy won the Washington SF Association Small Press Short Fiction Award for "Siren Beat" (also published by Twelfth Planet Press) in 2010.

Acknowledgements

My grateful thanks to Alisa for making such a collection possible, and for pushing me to expand the 'Agrippinaverse' into a greater thing than I had possibly imagined. I am excited to be part of the Twelve Planets project among so many amazing authors. Extra hugs and thanks to the many volunteers who help with the proofing and other odd jobs at TPP, and to Amanda for her excellent covers! You all make me look good.

Thanks to the University of Tasmania, particularly the Classics Department (and very specifically Dr Paul Gallivan), for providing me with the education I have so joyfully misused. All anachronisms, clangers and manticores contained within this text are my own responsibility.

I am supremely grateful to my honey, Andrew, for all of his support, to Kaia for her beta reading (not only a Swedish Writing Fairy but also a Lesbian Advisory Committee, all in the one person!), and to everyone who looks after my children while I am busy typing.

Finally, my apologies to Livia Drusilla Augusta for not allowing her to be a protagonist this time around, and instead handing an entire literary universe over to her upstart chit of a great-granddaughter. You are honestly still my favourite and my best.

What Are the Twelve Planets?

The Twelve Planets are twelve boutique collections by some of Australia's finest short story writers. Varied across genre and style, each collection will offer four short stories and a unique glimpse into worlds fashioned by some of our favourite storytellers. Each author has taken the brief of 4 stories and up to 40 000 words in their own direction. Some are quartet suites of linked stories. Others are tasters of the range and style of the writer. Each release will bring something unexpected to our subscriber's mailboxes.

When Are the Twelve Planets?

The Twelve Planets will spread over 2011 and 2012, with six books released between February and November each year.

The first three titles are *Nightsiders* by Sue Isle (March), *Love and Romanpunk* by Tansy Rayner Roberts (May) and *Thief of Lives* by Lucy Sussex (July).

How to Receive the Twelve Planets

The Twelve Planets will be available for purchase in several ways:

Single collections will be priced at $20/$23 International each including postage.

A season's pass will offer the three collections of the season for $50/$65 International including postage and each sent out on release, or on purchase of season's pass.

Full subscriptions to the series are $180/$215 International including postage and each sent out on release.

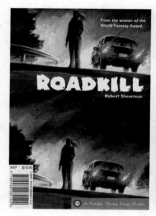 

Roadkill *Robert Shearman*
Siren Beat *Tansy Rayner Roberts*

A Twelfth Planet Press Double

Two novelettes—*Roadkill* by Robert Shearman and *Siren Beat* by Tansy Rayner Roberts—published in tête-bêche format form the first Twelfth Planet Press Double.

Roadkill is a squeamishly uncomfortable story with the kind of illicit weekend away that you never want to have.

Siren Beat is a paranormal romance sans vampires or werewolves but featuring a very sexy sea pony. A minor group of man-eating sirens on the docks of Hobart would not normally pose much of a challenge for Nancy, but she is distracted by the reappearance of Nick Cadmus, the man she blames for her sister's death.

Siren Beat
Winner of the WSFA Small Press Short Story Award
Roadkill
Shortlisted for British Fantasy Award for Best Novella

Horn *Peter M. Ball*

There's a dead girl in a dumpster and a unicorn on the loose. No-one knows how bad that combination can get better than Miriam Aster. What starts as a consulting job for city homicide quickly becomes a tangled knot of unexpected questions, and working out the link between the dead girl and the unicorn will draw Aster back into the world of the exiled fey she thought she'd left behind ten years ago.

Dead girls and unicorns? How warped can this get?

Locus Recommended Reading List

Shortlisted for Best Fantasy Novel and Best Horror Novel, Aurealis Awards

Bleed *Peter M. Ball*

For ten years ex-cop Miriam Aster has been living with her one big mistake—agreeing to kill three men for the exiled Queen of Faerie. But when an old case comes back to haunt her it brings a spectre of the past with it, forcing Aster to ally herself with a stuntwoman and a magic cat in order to rescue a kidnapped TV star from the land of Faerie and stop the half-breed sorcerer who needs Aster's blood.

Shortlisted for Australian Shadow Award for Best Long Work

Glitter Rose

Marianne de Pierres

The *Glitter Rose* Collection features five short stories by Marianne de Pierres—four previously published and one new story. Each copy of this limited edition print run is signed and presented in a beautiful hardbound cover, with internal black and white illustrations.

The *Glitter Rose* stories are set against the background of Carmine Island (an island reminiscent of Stradbroke Island, Queensland) where a decade ago spores from deep in the ocean blew in, by a freak of nature, and settled on the island. These spores bring fierce allergies to the inhabitants of the island. And maybe other, more sinister effects. As we follow Tinashi's journey of moving to and settling into island life, we get a clearer picture of just what is happening on Carmine Island.

Sprawl

Sprawl is an exciting new original anthology, glimpsing into the strange, dark, and often wondrous magics that fill the days and nights of Australia's endlessly stretching suburbs.

Liz Argall/Matt Huynh—Seed Dreams (comic)
Peter Ball—One Saturday Night, With Angel
Deborah Biancotti—Never Going Home
Simon Brown—Sweep
Stephanie Campisi—How to Select a Durian at Footscray Market
Thoraiya Dyer—Yowie
Dirk Flinthart—Walker
Paul Haines—Her Gallant Needs
L L Hannett—Weightless
Pete Kempshall—Signature Walk
Ben Peek—White Crocodile Jazz
Tansy Rayner Roberts—Relentless Adaptations
Barbara Robson—Neighbourhood Watch
Angela Slatter—Brisneyland by Night
Cat Sparks—All The Love in the World
Anna Tambour—Gnawer of the Moon Seeks Summit of Paradise
Kaaron Warren—Loss
Sean Williams—Parched (poem)

Locus Recommended Reading List

www.twelfthplanetpress.com